THE L

I stood at the bott... ... ...
the telephone. Joel ... ...
doubt still in bed. ... ...ng he a get that
special letter from me. What would he think of
it? I thought over what I'd written, and my
cheeks began to burn. If he left it lying about or
showed it to his friends...

To my dear daughter Charlotte, with love

THE LOVING GHOSTS

Josephine Poole

RED FOX

A Red Fox Book
Published by Random House Children's Books
20 Vauxhall Bridge Road, London SW1V 2SA

A division of Random House UK Ltd

London Melbourne Sydney Auckland
Johannesburg and agencies throughout
the world

First published in 1988
by Hutchinson Children's Books
Beaver edition 1989
Red Fox edition 1992

Set in Baskerville by BookEns,
Saffron Walden, Essex

Printed and bound in Great Britain by
Cox & Wyman Ltd, Reading, Berkshire
ISBN 0 09 959690 3

In my end is my beginning

I n love! That's how it all started. Obsession with the boy at the desk in front of mine, even to the lobes of his ears. Rapt contemplation of the miracle of his hands. Tongue-tied astonishment at the beauty of his voice, particularly when talking to me. Rapid development of relationship, with contingent plummetting of class marks except in poetry and playreading; amazement that the class can still exist round the glory that is Us. Kisses, embraces out of this world, supernaturally uniting us with everyone who has ever fallen in love—

Events at home were equally dramatic. Soon Mum and I were hammering away at each other every weekend, and often after school as well. When she suggested that I should spend Christmas with her sister Rose, instead of spoiling it for everyone at Granny's, she never expected me to agree, and that was why I said I would go, lit up with rage as I was at the time. I didn't consider it as a serious possibility. I thought I could count on Dad to persuade me against it, but I was wrong. He didn't even try, and that was a bitter twist, which made me realize how unpleasant home had got.

But soon I remembered that although Rose lived in the country, and was thought the epitome of spinsterishness by our family, she did a full-time job. It might well be easier to see Joel there, than to sneak out under Granny's eagle eye. We were bound to be separated over Christmas one way or the other, and I wasn't afraid of that; there would be letters and phone calls, and then he'd come down by motorway, or high speed train on which Mum and I now sat.

But as the distance increased between me and London, I

felt unexpectedly depressed. And the rain-sodden landscape was exactly tuned to the misery in my heart. My mother read her paper, observing me sometimes over her glasses. I could have avoided this by taking the seat next to her, but then we might have touched each other.

The couple next to us got out at Reading.

'You're not to try to see him,' she said then – apropos of nothing – straight out of the blue. 'I trust you.'

As far as I was concerned she hadn't spoken. I stared out of the window. She often won when we fought together, assuming moral superiority with no scruples about hitting below the belt. I didn't say what I thought – if you imagine you can control *his* actions, you're mistaken, and when he comes, *I shall see him*. There's not a thing you can do about that, Mother dear.

Next, by some quirk of the maternal brain, she thought of asking if I'd noticed Windsor Castle.

'No.'

'I should have reminded you to look out for it. It looks rather splendid from the train.'

No comment. Mental continuo: can it be that she really has no idea of what I'm going through? Is it possible that 'd' for dependable, debonair, doctor Dad was her first fortunate choice? I scowled surreptitiously at her. I had to admit that she looked, for her age, young and pretty. Why not? Thanks to Dad she could organize the household all her own way, treat herself to clothes and hairstyles whenever she liked, arrange the family holidays plus extra music lessons for her favourite person Tim my brother, run her own car. . . .

It was a slight accident with the Renault that had landed us on this train, denying me any privacy on a day when I was beginning to need it badly, and giving her a chance to be perky with the ticket collector, 'It's really a treat to go by train for a change. . . .' Tell that to the two thin girls struggling into our carriage with their toddlers and pushchairs, one-parent families probably, going somewhere for Christmas while the acid rain pours down.

'Have a sandwich.'

'No, thanks.'

'You must eat something.'

'Why?'

'Oh, come on, Christy! Stop sulking.'

'*I'm not hungry.*'

The taxi ride from the station had struck me as a danger point when she might let fly the parting shots. But it turned out that any home truths would include the driver, because it was an ordinary car without a partition. So we isolated ourselves in the corners of the back seat and she redid her make-up for the sister she didn't often see, whom she had bossed into having me for Christmas.

Aunt Rose lived right out of town, but we must have travelled double the distance because our driver couldn't find his way. He had to turn round twice, losing his temper and angrily accelerating. So this is agriculture I thought, staring out as we sloshed through puddles on the uneven road which presently became so narrow that Mum grew nervous. Brown rain here, instead of grey; mean little fields and drab hedges instead of mean little houses and drab streets.

'Not much of a day,' remarked our driver.

She agreed, and added, 'What happens if we meet a tractor round one of these corners?'

He answered by speeding round the next with his hand on the horn.

A cottage on the right, a high stone wall. Elaborate pillars topped with some sort of a bird, in stone; hanging incongruously between, a plain black iron farm gate with a letterbox wired to it. The box needed painting but the name was still legible: WADHAM'S.

'This is it,' growled our driver, braking abruptly, turning

in. Mum started fumbling in her bag. He got out and had difficulty opening the gate. She tapped on the window. 'Don't worry, we'll walk down, we haven't much luggage.' So he extracted what there was, she paid him, he drove away.

The gate had sunk on its hinges and had to be lifted away from the catch. A string of drops flew off as we pushed through. Down each side of the drive there were thick, dark yew bushes, irregularly spaced. Behind them, high walls cut off the view and, I supposed, the house. Only the drive, which needed gravelling, led forward to nothing one could see but the black yews, the grey sky.

Mother led the way briskly, gripping her bag under her elbow. I felt weak, shivery, thinned out by travelling. There was no wind, there were no birds. I could feel the coldness of the rain through my hair. We passed the secret bushes one by one. The only sounds were our footsteps, and the dripping of the rain.

Suddenly I felt afraid. I was about to be cut off, marooned! It was a plot arranged by Mum who walked hastily as if fearing that I might see through her at last. It was the sort of persecution that happens in nicely behaved, middle-class families (not Joel's): the artificially extended childhood that gives parents the right to go on imposing decisions. So – question time – why not drop the bags and run? What could Mummy do about that? Why stay obedient to the collar-and-lead routine? Character-revealing answers: I haven't a clue how to find the station. Besides – let's face it – I'm not sure how welcoming Joel's family would be.

So she led, and (with a bad grace) I followed.

A second pair of pillars on the left, topped with the same unidentifiable flying objects; another gate, the duplicate of that at the head of the drive but heightened at the top by a strip of wire netting. Mum's turn to tackle the fastening, while I stared across a weedy courtyard at the house. It was very tall, and huge, and ancient – not cherished antique, but grubby, crumbly ancient. Each of the long, narrow windows was stone mullioned and divided into many little panes, conveying a secretive, a barricaded look. Between the gables and high chimneys, the slate roofs wore the wet like a loose and glimmering skin. The plaster façade, originally ochre, had been often patched, and down it the rain ran from the brimming gutters, like tears down an old face.

Aunt Rose must have been looking out for us, for at that moment a side door opened and Mum, cooing, 'Here we are at last, the train took *hours*!' sped over the gravel to embrace her, while I sloped after, burdened and uncouth. Rose smiled palely at me and said, 'Christabel?' as though I might have been somebody else. 'How you've grown – I wouldn't have known you!'

'Why the barbed-wire entanglement?' I asked. She didn't seem to understand, so I pointed to the gate.

'Oh – Mrs Wadham's dogs. She keeps whippets. Oh dear, oh dear, you've left it open!'

I dumped my bags and went back to shut it. I knew that behind my back Mother was mouthing the details, '*very* upset – a complete break – sure to forget him –'

Rose ushered us inside and led the way down a dirty little passage. It ended in a swing door covered with dark felty material fastened with brass studs. We filed through into a larger, grander, not much cleaner passage which in turn opened into a lofty hall with a soaring mahogany staircase and several panelled doors, all shut. The only furniture was a stool in one corner with a telephone on it. Rose opened one of the doors and we went into a large sitting room with a tall, mullioned window at the end. The colours in this room were typically Rose, washed-out pinks and blues and greys, and there were several pieces of elegant furniture that

11

somehow looked like bits of sets, including three different chairs. There was a grand marble fireplace with a very small fire in it, recently lit, for damp clung. Mum crouched by the grate and put on more logs as soon as Rose had gone to fetch tea. A white marble head supported the mantelpiece; there was no way of telling whether it was a man or a woman, or whether the eyes were meant to be open, or closed.

'You ought to speak to Mrs Wadham about the woodworm,' Mum said when Rose returned with a tray. She often notices things I miss completely.

'Oh, she won't do anything about that,' said Rose, at once on the defensive. 'Why should she? She's old, she has no children. She's happy to let the place rot round her.'

'It's a pity to let it go.'

'It's rent free, I can't grumble.' The pot let out the tea in blobs and squirts.

There was a little alcove with shelves, made entirely of mirrors. I supposed it had been meant to display china. Now the shelves were empty, slips of ceiling caught in them, plaster roses and fleurs-de-lis. I imagined Joel's face severally reflected in the angled mirrors. I imagined him on one of the stiff chairs. I saw how he would dominate that room, being young and male and beautiful.

'Why don't you sit down?' asked Rose. She added, 'Don't worry, we can be cosy in the butler's pantry.'

'Why, is there a butler?'

She actually blushed then, and I was glad, I needed to torment someone and Rose was easy game. Mother snapped, 'Don't be crude, Christy!'

Silence.

'How are you going to pass the time while you're here?' Rose asked me doubtfully.

'I though you said on the phone that she could help in the shop,' said Mother.

'Well, but we aren't very busy at the moment, the weather's been so awful.'

'Perhaps it'll clear up. Anyway, Christy's very adaptable. She's used to amusing herself. She reads, draws. She can even cook.' Mum took more tea. 'And she's brought some schoolwork to do. You don't have to worry about her.' Thanks, thanks.

They continued a desultory conversation. I didn't want any tea. I walked about the room, stared out of the window at the view (grass sloping down to a line of trees and up again to mist-covered hills), stared at the pictures on the walls (woman with children; different woman with dogs; woman, different again, with man, husband presumably; man with short neck and small head showing off horse, ditto). I could see that it was difficult for my companions to ignore me. Several times Mum looked at her watch; the London train left at five. Rose was going to take her to the station and at last she went out of the room, fussing about the car keys.

'Are you coming to see me off?' Mother then asked me.

'No, I'll stay here.'

'Remember your promises.'

'I didn't promise anything!' This alteration of the facts enraged me. 'How can you tell such bloody lies?'

She was putting on her coat. She said, 'That's what I really disapprove of in your friend Joel. He's a bad influence on you. He's making you into a coarse, rough person. You aren't a bit like that really.'

'You haven't a clue what I'm like!'

'Don't be stupid!' The maternal calm was ruffling. 'I've known you for nearly sixteen years, that's long enough, I should think!'

'Quite long enough for me, anyway!'

Rose came back. She had heard us, or guessed we were

having words. She inched in at the door as if she was intruding. I wanted to push her; so did Mum from the way she flounced out. I noticed my bag and suitcase still in the hall. 'I'll unpack,' I said coldly. 'Where's my room?'

'Upstairs, the first on the right. The bed's made up, I put flowers,' Rose told me, placatingly.

'Goodbye then, Christy.' Mother was stern.

'Goodbye.' I started to climb.

'Remember, I trust you!'

I paused, glared down at her over the banisters. Foreshortened by the drop, she looked dolly squat, not up to the architecture or for that matter the situation, in her silly, careful country clothes that matched each other but certainly not this afternoon's impression of the great outdoors.

The keys in Rose's thin hand clinked apprehensively.

'I trust you to make the best of it,' Mother intoned.

Then they left through the baize door, as I called, carefully casual, 'Give Dad my love.'

But I shouldn't have let that out, because when I found my room there was nothing to do but sit down on the bed and cry. It was just the feeling of being away – abandoned over Christmas. Surely that's what fathers are for, to curb the ragings of mothers? Mine could have prevented this. It was the first time he'd let me down.

I heard Rose come back, but I didn't intend to leave my room. Later I heard feet on the stairs. I waited for the hesitant knock, the propitiating voice. I didn't get up or open the door.

'I'm afraid I always eat supper rather early. Would you like some scrambled egg?'

'No thanks. I'm not hungry. I'm going to bed.'

'All right, dear.' A note of relief in the voice? 'See you in the morning.'

'Okay.'

14

'Sleep well then. Good night.'

''Night.'

I went on with the letter I was writing to Joel. I'd printed the telephone number with the address at the top. I creased the paper with passionate kisses – not that I told him that, nor how I kissed the envelope all over.

Then I went to bed. I got out the book I'd brought to keep the diary of my exile, and wrote up day one.

It was difficult to concentrate on the diary. My mind kept running after Joel, recalling particularly his hands and lips, and imagining how it would be to go the whole way which we hadn't yet. I got myself very worked up, but strangely enough it was at this point that an inescapable drowsiness touched me, the book and pen fell from my grasp and I dropped off.

I fell suddenly, heavily asleep, into a tide surging mostly through dark dreamlessness, but every now and then I almost surfaced on a wave, when I was aware of a thin small noise, only before I could wake up properly I was drawn on again. Gradually it came to me that it was the whining of a dog, that one of Mrs Wadham's whippets had somehow got trapped in our part of the house, but every time I was about to haul myself out to do something about it, on I rolled. However, though it was not a loud noise, it was persistent. The creature seemed to sense that somewhere there was a sympathetic listener. The whining wasn't always from the same place, but sometimes closer, sometimes further, as if the dog was looking about for a human to let it out. And at last its diffident whine was very close indeed, right up to my bed, and then I did jerk awake, and sat bolt upright with my eyes open.

The room was full of moonlight. I could clearly see that no dog was there; I also saw that as my door was shut, no dog could have got in. And now I listened, listened, but heard nothing.

After a while I got out of bed and crept along the passage to the bathroom. On the way back, I paused by a half-open door, peered in. Rose was asleep in there, lying on her back with her long hair spread over the pillow. So thin she was, she hardly made a shape in the bed. Her faded day colours were sublimated to shades of pearl in the still room. The dressing-table mirror was all awash in the moonlight, as if it had abandoned its daytime duty of reflection.

The upstairs passage was transformed into a clerestory by the magical moon steeply beaming through its mullioned windows. In contrast, the shadowy stairs led down – to what? It didn't seem that they could connect with anything I had noticed on the ground floor. I shut myself silently into my room and went to the window. The leaded panes were covered all over with creeper, but at this time of year only a few withered leaves stuck, bunched against the glass. I looked down into the garden: a stretch of silver lawn cut off by a dark and shadowy wood, with a speckled high brick wall on one side, and a thick black hedge on the other. At the far end of the wall, on the left, there was an odd little brick building on two floors, like an overgrown sentry box. I thought, Joel and I will be able to hide in there – that was the idea that immediately came into my mind.

The shadows thrown by the wood were pierced by the moon which shone directly upon the summerhouse, and illuminating the two semi-circular steps under the little porch, showed that the door was standing open. What a place, what a place to hide! There were wads of foliage along the wall, some sort of evergreen, ivy probably, but a trick of the light turned them into roses, rambler roses in full bloom. I could imagine the smell of them as I wished myself with Joel down there in that enchanted garden. And all the while the moon was doing its conjuring upside down, because there it lay just underneath me in the garden pond – dead centre, dead white like the core of an exotic fruit.

I went back to bed with the clammy feeling you get when

you've stayed in the bath too long after the hot water supply has run out. No more dogs or dreams – I slept soundly till morning.

Next morning I woke early and lay for a while, thinking. It was good not to hear the scales which Tim practises before breakfast, alerting the household, precipitating a typical exchange in sharp voices between bedrooms, 'Really, Christy, it wouldn't hurt *you* to get up early for change!' 'Okay, but you might think of *Dad*! Nobody considers *him*!' 'Nonsense, he had to be up anyway. It's time you realized that Grade Eight at fourteen is exceptional – *very* exceptional –' While the trumpet unscrews the linings of my ears even through the pillow I cram over my head with clenched fists.

I considered spending the whole day in bed, but I decided against it. I wanted to post my letter. And there might be one for me, though it wasn't likely I'd hear so soon. Joel would hate putting pen to paper, he wasn't the writing sort. But he might turn up – he might turn up at any time. I thought about him, and soon my pulses were racing. My fantasies were interrupted by a plop, however, and opening my eyes, I observed a brown patch in the ceiling. Evidently it was raining again, and the roof leaked.

I heaved up on one elbow and confirmed yesterday's impression that there was no means of heating this room, apart from a pair of ornamental candles on the dressing table. I reached for my longest sweater and Tim's rugger socks, and padded along the passage to run a bath. The bathroom was very large and chilly, and I had to wedge the door with a chair. It contained odd things, such as a bookcase with old editions of the Bible and encyclopedias in it, and a hat stand which was useful for hanging clothes

19

on when, at the last minute, you nerved yourself for the plunge. The bath itself was made of iron, with blue and brown stains between the taps and the plug, and it had little iron legs, and feet in the shape of paws. The plumbing whistled and boomed. I felt surprisingly cheerful, and washed my hair. All the same it wasn't an experience to linger over, and I was downstairs, dressed, in record time.

Rose was already drinking tea in the butler's pantry. Last night's glamorous hair stood out brown and frizzy to her shoulders, and she had on a pale-blue flannel dressing gown that might have dated from her school days. She was older than my mother, but here and now she looked younger by years. There were writing things on the table. She was surprised and not, I suspected, entirely pleased to see me up so early. I sat down, and she passed me a mug of tea. The pantry had fitted cupboards and a sink; Rose had added a modern cooker and fridge, and there was still room for an armchair in front of the gas fire. Snug.

'I write all my letters before breakfast,' she told me. 'The way ladies used to in the last century.'

I couldn't think of anything to add to this, so I changed the subject. 'What time do you have to be at work?'

'I leave here at nine. What are you going to do with yourself all day? I mean, you can come in with me, but it's not very exciting when the shop's empty. . . . Of course we can't pay you when there's nothing for you to do.'

'What sort of shop?'

'Local crafts – candles like the ones in your bedroom, pot pourri, hand-woven scarves, that sort of thing. Usually we're quite rushed around Christmas, but this rain keeps people at home.'

'I'll stay here. Did you hear the dog last night?'

'*Dog*, Christy? I haven't got a dog.'

'No, I know. I thought it must be one of Mrs Wadham's

20

strayed in by mistake.'

'But there's no way in, Christy.' Rose was staring at me as if she couldn't make head or tail of this story. I said, 'Is there a fire I could have for my room?'

She was immediately distraught. 'Oh dear, I suppose you're used to central heating, and there's only the one old oil stove for upstairs, and I'm out of paraffin!'

'Isn't there an electric fire I could use?'

'No, no, the wiring's not safe. It's all pre-war, nineteen-thirties.' I had completely disrupted her early morning routine. She got up and began clearing away her writing things. 'What do you usually eat for breakfast?' she thought of asking, in a tone that somehow discouraged any idea of kippers, or bacon and eggs.

'Just toast and coffee.'

'Oh good, that's what I always have. Could you make it, do you think? I'll go and get dressed. Give me ten minutes.'

There were many small shelves in the butler's cupboards, and as I hunted for the breakfast things, I got an idea of Rose's magpie habits. Used labels and string, old Christmas cards, tokens for cheap offers, receipted bills – it seemed she never threw anything away. All was neatly arranged, clipped together or circled with a rubber band. All was clean, yet the cupboards had a funny smell; a sour, old, musty smell that would return no matter how often she scrubbed or sprayed. I burnt the toast while I was ferreting.

'Oh dear, oh dear,' she said, rushing in, her age again in flat heels and an ethnic two-piece. 'No – don't throw it away! I'll scrape it. No, only one slice for me, I'm late already. Did you heat the milk? Never mind, I haven't time. No, marmalade please, up there – not that one, the one above – never mind, I'll get it.'

She rushed off to work with a black toast crumb on her

cheek, that I didn't know how to mention. I went with her to the drive end, ostensibly to open gates, but I wanted to be first at the letter box – not that I expected anything for myself. And there wasn't. I noticed a public post box though, set in the wall close to the cottage. So as soon as Aunt Rose, bent forward with anxious concentration, gripping the steering wheel as if the little car might bolt, had got herself into the road and out of sight, I slipped in Joel's letter. The collection was in half an hour, so he should get it tomorrow.

A chilly, brown, dripping morning. I scurried back to the house, slamming gates as I went; bolted doors behind me as instructed; took the creaky old stairs two at a time; was out of breath and almost warm when I reached my bedroom. I looked out the novel I wanted to finish, and a history book in case I felt like working, and then I thought I would have a snoop round before I went downstairs, because it was too early to ring Joel, he would still be in bed.

There weren't many rooms upstairs because they were all so large, even the bathroom being bigger than our living room at home which is spacious by London standards. I discovered a huge broom cupboard – that's to say it had brushes and a mop in it, as well as dusty trunks and suitcases. I only peered in, because it had no window and the light didn't work. But I noticed (intriguing clue) a smart pale-blue zip-up bag with Rose's name in careful print, over an Italian address. This was a holiday venture that had escaped the family ear!

I went on to the room at the end of the passage. The paper was peeling off the walls and the rain sounded clearly through the roof. Dead leaves had blown in from somewhere and drifted into corners; the fireplace was choked with soot. I looked out of the streaming windows. I was so high up that even allowing for the hills opposite, the view included a lot of sky. A bird lay on the sill, a dead swallow. It had died with its wings spread against the glass. I didn't touch it. The putty holding in the panes had turned crumbly, and looked more like moss; in places rainwater was spurting in. Then I noticed that someone had written on one of the panes. The date was there – 1939 – and the same word scratched, again and again: LOVE it said and LOVE and LOVE and LOVE and LOVE.

I don't know how much effort it takes to write on glass, I've never had a diamond to do it, but that word so deeply etched, so often repeated, looked passionate. It made me wonder how it had ended. The bird seemed to symbolize mortality. I wondered how many flights to Africa it had made, and now it lay here; it had survived the hazards of those journeys, to be trapped in summer by a pane of glass.

Behind me the dead leaves shifted, catching a draught. It was easy to imagine skirts rustling, light feet in the passage, as the old house creaked and the rain hissed down. And the weather wouldn't clear for a bit, I could see waves of it, all wet, coming from the hills. I turned my back and wondered how this room had been furnished when the girl – surely it had been a girl – wrote with her ring on the window. There was nothing left to show. But in a way that was good, because the construction of the building was beautiful. The vine-patterned wallpaper in the passage was too faded now to detract from the stone-mullioned windows, or the carved wooden door frames, or the graceful mahogany staircase. The house was like an old beauty reduced to the last shreds of Dior in her wardrobe – not disgraced, but with a melancholy dignity.

I went back to the kitchen, put my books and transistor on the table with the breakfast things, crossed the hall to the telephone, dialled Joel's number. According to my calculations he would be up, but not yet out. My heart beat sickeningly as I waited for him to answer, and wondered how I would ask for him if he didn't. Disapproval of our relationship is not, let me explain, all on my parents' side. As it turned out I needn't have worried – the bell rang and rang, but nobody was at home. I put down the receiver and returned to the kitchen, made myself more coffee, opened a book.

When the phone did ring a few minutes later, I literally jumped in my chair. My heart bounced into my throat as if I'd swallowed a squash ball. I flew across the hall, snatched the receiver.

'Hallo?' My voice sounded odd, husky.

Rose.

'I tried before, but the line was engaged. Was someone trying to get me?'

My mind moved like lightning, over the disappointment.

'Somebody rang, but I didn't get to the phone in time.'

'Oh dear. Oh well, if it's important, they'll try again. I forgot to tell you about your lunch.'

'Yes?'

'There's an egg, and some cheese in the fridge. Can you manage on that?'

'Sure.'

'I'll bring something back with me for supper.'

'Okay.'

'I'll have to go now, here's a customer. Don't waste the gas. 'By-ee.'

''Bye.'

I turned from the phone, sick at heart. I'd been so sure that that was going to be Joel. It was hard not to feel that he had let me down.

As I stood there feeling miserable, someone in the next door part of the house started to play the piano – a few arpeggios just to warm up the fingers, a chord or two, and

24

then 'Moon River', an old jazz tune. It wasn't any sort of a performance; this player was doodling, thinking about something else, and after a nostalgic wander with 'Moon River', embarked on 'Tea for Two' with several wrong notes. I imagined a girl, a 'thirties girl, following these old-fashioned tunes while she looked out of the window; only for her it wasn't raining – because that music went with sunshine and girls who didn't work, but were not 'unemployed'. The piano sounded clear, but not loud – it couldn't be in the next large room, perhaps the large room beyond that. If it was Mrs Wadham, she didn't play like an old lady.

I went back to the kitchen and looked in the fridge. I found three eggs and the cheese, and made myself an omelette. Over the meal I completed the crossword Rose had begun in yesterday's newspaper. Then I read. It was a pleasant if negative way of passing the time, and even warm with the door closed and the gas fire full on. I surfaced now and then to make more coffee. When I finished my novel I saw that it had stopped raining, there was even a gleam of sunshine in the little yard outside the kitchen window, and I decided to go for a walk. I got my coat, and locked up the house (Rose had left particular instructions). I thought I would try to find the garden I could see from my bedroom, so I turned left at the first gate, away from the road.

The high brick walls continued along each side of the drive, and the yew bushes grew closer together and more thickly, as if they had never been trimmed. Laurels had been planted to fill any gaps, so on a wet day this neglected stretch was very dark and dank and dripping. The drive soon dwindled to a muddy path, and the weed grasses soaked my legs to the knees. I would have turned back, but now I saw that the walls must come to an end just ahead, for two more of the stone flying creatures were just visible above the yews. So I pushed on, drenched and breathing hard, and presently I was encouraged by red paint gleaming between the branches. Soon I found a stone archway fitted with a pair of tall painted wooden doors, which must be the entrance to somewhere. It was a long time since anyone had gone that way, for grass and brambles tangled against them, and where they stopped, ivy took over. I jiggled the iron fastening, and gave one of the doors a shove. To my surprise, it creaked and gave, and then I shoved with all my strength until I had a gap wide enough to squeeze through.

Inside was a cobbled farmyard, surrounded by low buildings where animals had once been kept. Now windows and doors, even roofs gaped, and ivy was almost the only living thing to thrive there. Almost – because while I was staring about, I heard a cough behind me, and turning sharply saw some calves in a pen in the closest of the sheds. The sound and smell of them reminded me at once of our happiest family holidays, which had been spent on a farm. This was long ago, when Tim and I were a pair and Mum and Dad knew their place and had not yet recognized our talents. But we were very young then.

All this time the sky was clearing, and the afternoon sun was warm though the air was colder. The old roofs glittered and the drips, catching the light, flashed as they fell from slates or broken gutters. There was a small orchestra of watery effects, one way and another; but the most persistent seemed to come from under my feet, and that was disconcerting, until I connected it with a paving stone set into the cobbles with a heavy iron ring in it. I realized then that there must be a large well or cistern down there, filling up after the rain. I could hear the rushing, gurgling water echoing in a stone cavity.

I was still crouching by the stone, listening, when I heard the rumble of a tractor approaching. As I stood up, wiping my hands on my trousers, an ancient machine rattled round the corner, hauling a box with some bales of straw in it. It crashed to a stop at the sight of me, and the driver glared as if it was an extraordinary thing to see anyone else on the farm. He jumped down and humped up a bale on to his shoulder, and then he said, 'Who the hell may you be?' He had a country accent, drawing out the vowel sounds.

'I'm staying at the house,' I said.

He turned and went in to the calves, stood the bale in a corner, took out his pocket knife and slit through the string with a quick movement. Then he straightened and stared at me again, pushed back his greasy cap and scratched his head. His face looked older than his hair which was curly and dark, though streaked with grey. 'Wadham's, d'you mean?' he asked. 'Is that where you're staying? With Mrs Wadham?' And he sounded as though that was the most extraordinary thing he had ever heard.

'Next door. With Rose Turner, if you know her. She's my aunt.'

'Ah,' he said. And he finished staring, and began shaking out the straw into the pen. 'Isn't she a caretaker of some sort?' he asked, without turning round.

'She lives in part of the house. She looks after everything when Mrs Wadham goes away.'

'Ah, but then she don't, do she?' he said, his face twisting with a knowing expression.

'How do you mean?'

'Go away. Mrs Wadham ain't gone away for years. Not with her arthritis.' He climbed over the rail to spread the straw. He said, 'Maybe she just likes to have somebody about. 'Tis a lonely old place on your own.'

'Yes, it is.'

The tractor had been chugging away all this time. He got back into it and slammed it into gear. I shouted, 'Is it okay if

I look round for a bit?'

'You can't hurt nothing!' He nodded, and drove away.

I wanted to look at the building across the yard. It was in better repair than the others, and I guessed it had been a stable; it was long, with several windows and doors – the sort of place that would have Mother transfixed in one of her three-minute-ecstacies (wouldn't that *convert*!). Most of the buildings round the yard were one-storey, but this had a loft with an odd little doorway where hay had been chucked in and out, long ago. I thought at first that it was all locked, and probably still in use as a store, but when I walked round the corner I found a wide opening where carts might once have been kept. There were bits of implements lying about, and an old turnip-chopper stood in a corner. I went on through an inner door, into the stable itself.

Somebody's pride and joy, once upon a time – even now it was beautiful. The stalls were still intact, separated by gracefully curved, panelled partitions, each with its hay rack and manger and enamelled plate on which was painted the name of the occupant. I walked up the cobbled passage, reading, dreaming – Topper, The Duke, Florence, Snowball, Flash. (Mine was Florence, a bay with a fine head, spirited but sensible. 'She'll look after you,' the groom said as I sprang lightly into the saddle.) But the windows were clouded with dust, even the rat holes looked empty. A corner of the ceiling had collapsed, leaving the laths sticking out like the ribs of a dead animal.

There were doors long bolted and barred leading into the yard, and another inner door into the harness room. Here racks and pegs stuck out of the walls, and a glass-fronted cupboard hung crookedly over the fireplace. A saddle balanced on one of the pegs, mouldering slowly in the damp, gradually shedding its stuffing. The peg was no longer at right angles to the wall and one day – tomorrow, in a month – it would no longer hold the saddle which would tumble with a crash to join the other bits lying where they had fallen – pieces of harness, a shattered pane of glass. . . . The display cupboard contained a number of crumpled ribbons carefully pinned in lines, faded to the colour of old newspaper. It suddenly struck me that these were rosettes – symbols of achievement, asterisks on the riding schedule.

The harness-room ceiling was low, only just out of my reach. In the far corner, a rough wooden ladder rose perpendicularly into the black opening of the loft. I could have climbed up there, and had a look. I didn't. For it was as if the chilly darkness in the loft began oozing down into the room. All at once the place began to feel like a tomb. Something had happened here, something momentous, some stroke of doom. And as if to underline that thought, the door leading into the stable suddenly clapped shut. Immediately, half the light was cut off. Now I couldn't see properly into the corners, or quite make out what the shapes were, hanging on the walls. I moved to the inner door but it wouldn't budge, it was solid as a gravestone, I was trapped!

The loft creaked, a small noise like a sigh. Whatever it was that threatened, came from there – I was unreasoningly sure of that. I was aware of a state of urgency building up around me. I don't know how else to put it. But it was as though the little room had a message for me, and I didn't want to receive it, not at all. I began to feel drawn out, weak, faint; my face felt odd, as though it belonged to someone else. I clamped my teeth over the insides of my lips to pull myself together – I mustn't lose control – if I did there would be no holding back! *No holding back what?*

There was a second door and it must lead into the yard. I clutched the handle, tried to turn it with both hands, noticed the key, twisted and wrenched at it, my breath battling with my thumping heart. It clicked and the door opened, giving me a crack on the knee. I fell out into the puddly yard with the slate roofs shining in the sun.

When I felt calmer I looked back. I could see that the room was just an ordinary, shabby little room with the light from the yard shining in. There was no accounting for the fact that I was still scared and shaky. I closed the door and looked at my watch and saw that it was nearly four. I went back into the house to wait for Rose.

I made some coffee and sat for a long time at the kitchen table in what Mum would have called a stupor (do get a move on, Christy!). But I was trying to rationalize my fright with some impromptu self-analysis. And soon I understood that it was the strangeness of having been transplanted that was making me overreact. My normal life was surrounded by purpose, even if it was mostly other people's, even if I often resisted it. Usually I had a string of occupations – buses to catch, meals to eat, lessons to learn. But all this had abruptly, completely changed. I wasn't used to having time on my hands. I had no experience of dilapidation, cobwebbed emptiness. So that explained – everything.

Amateur psychology is such a comfort, when there isn't really a problem.

My relieved mind returned to its favourite groove then, and I imagined Joel writing me a letter, or maybe it was only a card. His hand dwarfed the pen, showed it up as a cheap plastic job – he'd have looked more himself painting me a poster, or chipping out a message with a flint. His arm had golden hairs, and several tiny moles, the same size and colour as the spots you sometimes see on the brown shell of an egg. I watched him taking out an envelope, carefully copying my new address, but there were snags to the stamping and posting of it. It would mean a visit to the post office, and I couldn't picture him in a Christmas queue. He was too impatient. He would leave it for later, and it would be lost. And I could hear him saying, when we met, 'But I

30

did write!' He would sound injured, he would expect that much effort to have been enough, and so it was, at any rate it would do until post time tomorrow morning.

Rose came back with a little parcel containing our supper, and not much of it – two thin slices of Gala pork pie, for a treat, she said, because usually she had an egg. She was not pleased to discover that I had finished the eggs, and the cheese and most of the bread. 'I can see you're going to eat me out of house and home,' she said fretfully.

'I thought Dad was paying for my keep.'

She didn't deny it. She compressed her lips and didn't answer.

As I climbed the stairs to early bed, I felt suddenly, horribly lonely. No one had rung to see how I'd settled – and by no one, I meant Mum or Dad. I didn't really expect Joel to feel he had to rush to the phone, or Tim for that matter – most boys don't react like that, even when they're missing someone. But parents. . . . Mine should be worrying in case I ran away, or took a fancy to jump off the roof. They were altogether too optimistic.

Next morning I woke up early and wrote Joel a letter. I told him how much I was missing him, and why. I hoped his mother wouldn't find it, but if she did, even if she showed it to Mum, I didn't care. It was time my nearest and dearest took me seriously. My letter was explicit: absence couldn't make my heart grow fonder, but it did make it articulate.

It struck me at breakfast that Rose looked preoccupied, and I didn't have to wait long before, with her back turned, she broached the subject.

'I'm afraid I'm always out on Tuesday evenings. Will you be all right on your own?'

What choice did I have? 'How late will you be?'

'Oh, not late – about half-past nine. Do you want more toast?' We were in better time this morning.

'Okay, thanks.'

'It's the last slice.'

'You have it.'

'No, no, I want you to have it.' She needed to appease the twinge of guilt she felt about going out and leaving me behind. Rose's conscience was a tricky article.

It was fine, but a lot colder this morning. The puddles reflected little cold skies all the way up the drive. I saw her out, posted my letter and tremblingly looked in the Wadhams box. Nothing for me – again, nothing for me.

Then I couldn't breathe for a minute, as if I'd been winded. But really it wasn't important, it didn't mean anything! Joel hated writing – I should know! We were at school together. . . . This morning, had he been waiting eagerly for the postman? Grabbed my letter, hurried to a secret place, hungrily torn it open? Or was it a different scene?

His mother, 'There's a letter for you.' Turning it over. 'Country postmark. I should think it's that girl.'

Joel (yawning), 'Which girl?'

Takes letter, opens it while family continues the business of breakfast. Reads while pushing fingers through hair (typical beloved gesture). Smiles.

I walked unseeingly down the drive, back into the house. I went upstairs and sat down on my bed. I felt sick, I missed him so much. Next door the pianist struck up with a flourish of arpeggios. The notes sounded clearly through the mostly empty house. I didn't want another concert. I didn't want to read, either, it wasn't that sort of day. I pulled on another sweater, found my money, went downstairs. Halfway down I noticed the telephone. The arpeggios merged into the usual 'thirties selection. I dialled our home number, heard my mother's voice repeating it in warm, well-fed, socially-aware and suddenly astonishingly desirable number 5, Greenfields Close.

'It's freezing here, and I'm starving,' I snapped without preamble.

'Christy!' I seemed to be the person she most longed to hear. 'Love, how are you? I tried to get you yesterday but there was no reply. What were you and Rose up to? Out on the razzle?'

'Not likely, there's nothing to do. There's nothing to eat either, and it's cold as hell.'

'Is Rose there?'

'No, she's working.'

'But she must feed you! Look, I'll ring her tonight – what time does she go to bed? We'll be a bit late back after Tim's carol concert.'

'Don't worry, we'll get it sorted out. I'm angry, that's all.

In a mood. Be glad you're not here.'

'Well, find something constructive to do. Have you done any work?'

'No.'

'Please try. Your report wasn't all that good.'

'I know, I know. Don't go on about it.' Pause. 'There's this person next door will keep playing the piano. It gets on my nerves.'

'What person?'

'I don't know. Mrs Wadham, I suppose.'

'I thought she was crippled with arthritis.'

'Not in her hands, if it's her. Can't you hear?' And I held out the receiver in the direction of the dividing door.

'No, I can't hear anything. What's she playing?'

' "I Get a Kick Out of You". They're really old tunes.'

'It's nice she's so cheerful. Have you met her yet?'

'No. I don't think Rose goes round there much.' And we chatted on. It was the most amiable conversation we'd had for weeks.

Towards the end she said, 'You could join us for Christmas.'

'I'm okay.'

'Well, ring if you change your mind. You've got Granny's number. Now tell me what you're going to do today.'

'Don't know.' Access of weariness. 'Go for a walk probably. Open things for lunch. Rose's tins are all small, you need three for a meal. What are you doing?'

'Christmas shopping, but I've nearly finished. I got Granny a rug, rather a gloomy tartan, they said it was made in the Isles.'

'Which ones?'

'I don't know – Hong Kong, probably.'

We put down our receivers at last, full of affection. And my phone rang again at once. My heart leapt because possibly – but I could have guessed it would be Rose. Some uncanny intuition warned her when I was adding to the phone bill.

Red-hot Rose. I held her at arm's length, mumchance so she would think the phone was out of order. She quacked on for several minutes but even the piano was silent. Finally she said she would get the operator to check the line, and put down the receiver. I replaced mine and went into the kitchen and found things to eat. I felt better after that, and read the newspaper she had brought back with her yesterday. Afterwards I decided to go for another walk, in case there was a shop handy. I hid the key in a hole in the wall – there were several to choose from – and turned up the drive towards the road. I glanced into the mailbox just in case there was a second post though I was sure there wasn't (and there wasn't), and went left past the high wall and the cottage. Hearing the clunk of a chopper on wood, I looked over the hedge, and recognized the man I had met in the farmyard. He was trimming logs and chucking them into a basket. He raised his head and saw me, and asked whether it was cold enough for me.

'Yes, thanks! Do you think it'll snow?'

'Hope not! Don't want none of that horrible stuff!'

I was about to walk on when he threw down his little axe and came up to the gate. 'How long 'm you staying?'

'I'm not sure – over Christmas, anyway.'

'Don't you get lonely in that big house on your own?' His blue eyes were shrewd, and kindly. He saw at once that his words touched me. He said, 'You can always call in here, mind. There's always someone at home.'

'Thanks.'

'You 'm only a kid when all's said and done.'

Then somebody shrieked, 'Peter!' from the cottage, and a little blonde girl came running into the garden. So he returned to his wood, and I went on.

On each side of the road there were hedges, every so

35

often broken by a gate. Behind the hedges there were fields, sometimes a little wood. Occasionally the road divided, to the left or right, and then a signpost pierced the monotony, with directions to villages even more in the back of beyond, with names like places in a nursery rhyme. Catfoot was one, I remember. 'As I was going up Catfoot Hill, I met a man who kept a mill.' There is a darkness in these baby rhymes, a sinister element, a hint of hidden, adult meanings. Not far away the man with all the cats and wives was lurking, and the crooked man, and the woman who lived inside a hill.

I walked for miles. The only thing that passed me was a scarlet post office van, and apart from the driver I didn't see anybody, or pass a human habitation. And that felt very strange, because it was Christmas Eve the day after tomorrow, and in all my life this had been a time of shopping, cooking, cards, presents – panic dashes to the chemist's for talc for a forgotten aunt (sometimes Rose), to the post office with huge expenditure on stamps to ensure an impossibly quick delivery. A time of amnesty in the home – domestic quarrels forgotten, or postponed; a time of grandmothers and cousins. What was I doing here?

There was frost in the grass along the hedge, and a scouring wind. The fields were empty, the animals had been taken into shelter. No birds sang. The only sounds were my feet on tarmac, the rustle of dry leaves in the hedge. I don't know which way I went. Eventually, for no particular reason, I turned and walked back. And because I crossed the road to face the oncoming traffic (not that there was any), I noticed a little signboard pointing over a gate which said, 'Footpath to Wadham's'.

I stopped and looked over. The path showed clearly across the first field, as far as a stile into a wood. It seemed much pleasanter than tramping along the road. So I climbed the gate. I came to an old railway cutting, invisible from the road, between the field and the wood. It was all grassed over, and the embankments were thickly brambled – a marvellous place for blackberries in autumn. There were other trees in the wood beside pines, and several large black birds were flapping about among the top branches, rooks I suppose. I noticed a faint, sweet smell – not the cedary kind you'd expect in a wood at Christmas time, but flowery. It made me think how beautiful it would be here in the spring with Joel, when the bluebells were out.

I had one or two twists of flap, because the colours of the sky were beginning to deepen, and I was afraid there might be two Wadhams and I was going in the wrong direction. But the path was clear enough, and after crossing a couple more fields it led down to a river, and I saw the roofs and chimneys of the big house in the distance. Then I climbed down the bank, and washed my hands and face in the icy water. The evening seemed to creep up a step, just while I was doing that. The details of the landscape grew more precise, as if the cold outlined them with a black edge, or as if they were making a stand against the onset of darkness.

Soon I had an uninterrupted view of Mrs Wadham's part of the house. It was bigger than ours, more desolate with most of the windows palely shuttered like blind eyes. As I was watching, a light went on in a bay window downstairs, and I thought that a figure moved in that room, though it was the width of the field away. Some rooks flew ahead of me, into a wood of spindly trees at the top end of the field. Then I spotted the pointed roof of the odd little sentry box I could see from my bedroom window. But I was careful to keep to the path – if Mrs Wadham chanced to notice me she couldn't complain to Rose that I was trespassing.

Suddenly I saw that there was a man just ahead, very close to me. He was standing on the bank above the stream, staring across towards the hills. He was so still that I had an idea he might be shooting, or fishing; I didn't know about country sports, but he was dressed all in brown, as it might be for camouflage. He had on a tweed cap and jacket, mountaineer-type breeches tucked into heavy countrified socks folded over below the knee, laced shoes. He was all of a piece with the brownish grass along the bank, the wintry trees; I might have bumped into him with a few minutes less of light. As it was, I stopped dead, not seeing how I could avoid him, and feeling awkward in case after all I was in the wrong place, but at that moment he turned abruptly and set off across the field towards the house. We were so close that we could have touched each other, yet he didn't see me. I knew that he didn't.

I stood by the river, completely at a loss, appalled by the expression on his face. It was an expression of absolute despair. The people I knew never looked like that. I stared helplessly after him; his active figure was already lost between the river and the wood. For evening was closing in quickly now, it would be difficult to pick my way across the farmyard. And still I lost time standing there undecided, fussing when certainly there was nothing I could do.

I realized that I would have to leave the path to find my own way back, remembering the layout of my bedroom, and that the wood and summerhouse were in the wrong direction. So I hurried across the field. The lit bay window told me where Mrs Wadham must be, and I thought it would be safe to walk by the front, where the shutters were all closed. But I was just passing one of the large ground floor windows, when I heard the harsh sound of the shutter being pulled back. Immediately I dropped to my knees, cowered against the wall; inches above my head the window grated open. It was Mrs Wadham. She didn't see me. She leant out, over the stone sill, so close that the end of her mohair stole touched my face. I thought she must hear the hammering of my heart. She seemed to be staring down over the field, concentrated, motionless.

'Simon?' she said, not loudly. 'Are you there?' An old woman's voice, that still hoped.

I longed to say yes, he's here, he'll be with you in a minute. Of course I didn't, I'd hidden myself automatically and if I bobbed up now I'd probably give her a heart attack. But I was glad he was on his way.

She stared out for what seemed a long time. My joints felt as if they would start screaming. But at last she pulled the window shut and I heard the shutter crash into place. Then I hobbled on as fast as possible, anxious to get indoors before it became pitch dark.

I managed to find a way across the farm, and located the key after a panicky search. I had an unpleasant fumble and stumble to the baize door, not knowing where the light switch was, but once inside the house I turned on as much electricity as I could find. Then I scuttled upstairs for my drawing things, and down again to the kitchen. Too long to wait for Rose! Three hours at least, perhaps to music – perhaps Simon was the pianist. Perhaps he was a relation, staying over Christmas. Something terrible must have happened to him; perhaps he lived here now, Mrs Wadham had taken him in.

Perhaps, perhaps. I wanted Rose. I longed for company, conversation, even tv to collar the empty hours and bring them to heel. Too many empty rooms! Imagining Simon at the piano, I'd have been glad to hear it, but all was silent. I found a packet of soup and some anchovies and made a curious meal. *Too many empty rooms*; too many inaudible feet on the stairs, in the passages. If only Rose had tv – but I had to admit that whatever she'd got or hadn't, her nerves were stronger than mine. I opened my book, sharpened some pencils, tried to concentrate on this evening's project – 'Portrait of Joel'.

But it wouldn't come. It was constantly interrupted by the mouth and eyes of the man I had seen by the river.

I won't say that Rose looked different when she came in. She was as fussy as ever: how had I managed through the day, she'd tried to ring about what I was to eat for lunch, she had tried, but the phone seemed to be out of order though they'd said there was nothing wrong with it when they'd checked. Etc. etc. But she couldn't hide a glow of secret satisfaction: her evening had been a success. And that was when I knew that Rose had a gentleman friend. When you're in love, you can usually spot the symptoms in somebody else.

'Did you have a good time?' I asked. It was a perfectly normal question. There was no need for her to take cover behind the empty anchovy tin in the sink.

'Oh Christy, how could you?' The wail sounded genuine – maybe it was. 'I was saving those! What else did you find?'

'Only a packet of soup. I've got to eat!'

'*Not* my shrimp bisque?'

'It might have been, it was fishy. It had a gritty taste.'

'You didn't cook it long enough! You have to cook bisque for twenty minutes. You didn't even bother to read the instructions!'

'Sorry, *sorry*! I couldn't find anything else. Can I have some bread?' She had unpacked a small loaf from one of her cagey parcels.

'Well, all right, but don't finish it.' And she stowed away a little piece of cheese and some eggs before I could get at them. I ate the crust, and decided to force her hand.

'So how was your evening?'

'Oh, quite nice, thank you.' Back to me, busy in the fridge. Quelling tone.

'What did you do?'

'Not much, just sat and talked. Rather dull really.'

'What about?' The way I look at it, if you take in your niece to stay, it isn't polite to go on with your life as if you were alone. There are social obligations.

'Oh – books and things. And if you want to know which books, Thomas Hardy and the Wessex novels. Now are you satisfied?' She looked round and up at me – she was still crouching by the fridge. 'Do you think you will be staying over Christmas?'

I was completely taken aback. 'I thought that was the arrangement!'

'Well, yes, but obviously if you aren't happy you mustn't stay.'

'Who says I'm not happy?'

'Well, you must be very lonely on your own all day.'

'I'm okay. You said how it would be, and then you'll be having some time off.'

'Well, yes, but of course I always spend Christmas Day with a friend.'

This really cut the ground from under my feet. She wasn't the first person not to want me. Flash concept – huge charity poster, abandoned dog with caption, 'Won't you give Christy a good home this Christmas?' At the same time I was terrified that what she'd said was actually going to make me cry. I said furiously, 'You should have sorted that out before!'

'Of course you can come too if you want to.' Rose sounded pained. 'It's just that I'm afraid you'd be bored.'

I didn't answer. I collected my drawing things, my fingers were shaking.

'You'll have to tell me soon whether you want to stay or

not, because of the catering,' she persisted.

'I should think I'll stay, since you fixed it with Mum. Weeks ago.'

'Oh good,' she said, without conviction.

In the circumstances I didn't hope to make much of an exit, but being flustered I dropped my drawing as I was going through the door, and Rose picked it up for me. She looked at it before handing it back – just as Mum would have done – and she said, 'Oh!' in surprise, and looked more closely. Then she said, 'I didn't know you could draw like that.' And she looked at me with a new respect, which I had seen before in people's faces, and don't care about. They forget that it's a talent I was born with; I don't need Mother to remind me that it isn't an achievement like Timothy's playing. I haven't begun to work at it; perhaps I never will.

'Is it him?'

I understood that she meant Joel. I muttered, 'Not really.'

'I suppose you'll go on to Art School.'

'I don't know.'

'Oh, you must, it would be a crime not to! Such a waste.'

'I'm going to bed now, anyway.'

But I returned her good night, which I wouldn't have done five minutes earlier.

It was freezing upstairs. I hoped she'd lagged the hot water system. The cold was down to a trickle, and the loo wouldn't flush properly. Before I got into bed I looked out of the window. The man called Simon was standing in the garden, in the middle of the frosty lawn. He was staring at the summerhouse. The night was so lavish with moonshine, I had the illusion of shrubs in full leaf, flowers in full bloom.

He hadn't changed his clothes, or put on an overcoat.

Perhaps he hadn't gone into the house after all. Perhaps he was a manic depressive, that was why Mrs Wadham had called so anxiously for him. . . . In fact there was an obvious oddness about him, a picture-puzzle peculiarity – spot the deliberate mistake – but I couldn't pin it down.

I don't know how long he stood there. I changed into my nightclothes and some jumpers, and bitterly made up my diary in bed.

It struck me next morning that I'd definitely lost weight. Fringe benefit of Rose's starvation housekeeping – to be able to do up my jeans without losing my balance, gloat gloat. I was sharply interrupted by a long ring at the bell and pounding on the door, which echoed through the passages and up the staircase, and drew Rose from her Victorian idea of correspondence to answer it on hasty feet, while I followed as quickly as possible.

The impatient postman had already gone, leaving a huge parcel addressed to both of us, enough to ensure a bumper Christmas, with a batch of letters tucked under the string. I reached past Rose and removed them, which was easily done for she was pecking at the parcel. And my heart too was going rat-a-tat, but for a different reason, as I leafed through the envelopes – three cards for me from girlfriends, forwarded from home – and a letter, *a letter*!

From Dad.

Rose was all of a twitter. 'It's from Mum,' I said roughly. 'Don't you recognize her writing?' I looked through the envelopes again, more carefully.

'Oh dear, and I only sent her bath pearls!' Rose was flogging herself as usual.

'She likes them.'

'It *was* a gift pack. Do you think if I caught the post with some chocolates for New Year. . . ? Or a token. Would Timothy like a record token?'

'Don't bother, it doesn't matter! He gets heaps of things.'

My mind was like a desert, grey, empty; my mouth tasted

of dust. Part of the bitterness was knowing how I would build it up again, the love between Joel and me. Soon I would persuade myself with the old excuses – he was busy, he was disorganized; by tonight he would be back in his role of Christy's Great Lover. Oh I knew how it would be, and I despised myself, for after all there was no dodging the fact that if he felt love at all in the way I did, he would ring or write or come. But I was parched, and a mirage was better than nothing.

In the usual way I would have loved hearing from Dad, who hardly ever writes letters. He told me to phone if I changed my mind about staying with Rose and he'd drive down and fetch me. Otherwise it was a dry list of seasonal social events – school nativity play, Christmas parties at the hospitals, drinks with neighbours, etc – things neither he nor I rave over. He said home wasn't the same without me.

At breakfast Rose announced, deeply blushing, that she would tell her friend, that jealously guarded secret, to expect both of us on Christmas Day, and she offered me the ham in the fridge for lunch, so Mum's generosity was evidently working on her better nature. Then she rushed off. I was mean and didn't go with her to open the gates. From the bathroom window I watched her struggling, her grey and blue skirts wind-wrapped round her anxious legs.

Another very cold but clear day. I stood at the bottom of the stairs and stared at the telephone. Joel was only nine digits away, no doubt still in bed. This morning he'd get that special letter from me. What would he think of it? I thought over what I'd written, and my cheeks began to burn. If he left it lying about or showed it to his friends—

I went into the kitchen and messed about, washing up, sweeping the floor and so on. I made deadlines for Joel: he'll be sure to ring by ten o'clock, quarter past, half past, because he'll have to react to that letter. But he didn't. I could have hated him for his silence. I found something to read and turned the oven full on as well as the gas heater – Rose would have shrieked – and still I felt wretchedly cold. I wrapped up my feet in some drying-up towels and read on grimly; it was one way of passing the desert day. But still he hung about, nudging my concentration, and at every pause, whenever I blew my nose or made a cup of coffee, he clouded my mind.

Around midday the piano started up next door. The same old tunes, played in exactly the same way including errors – if it was a practice, the performer wasn't making any improvement. I hoped it was Simon. It was nice to think that there were other people in this pile of crumbling masonry besides me and Mrs Wadham.

Then I wanted to walk through and listen. If it was Simon, he might be glad to have company. I could introduce myself and say how much I liked hearing him play. We might have a conversation. And then I thought – Rose is right, I'm lonely, that's what's the matter with me. It's totally mad to trespass into somebody's house just to talk to a total stranger, in the usual way I wouldn't consider it, but I'm terribly lonely. And I went back to my book. But soon I remembered how miserable *he'd* looked – as if there was no hope for him in this world. I might be able to cheer him. It couldn't be much fun for him, Christmas with one old lady.

All this time, 'Moon River' was winding itself round my heart.

I got up and went into the hall. The door through into Mrs Wadham's was fastened with a bolt on our side, and there was also a keyhole, but no key. I crouched and put my eye to it but I couldn't see anything, so I imagined the key was in the other side and it was locked. Expecting this, I didn't hesitate about pulling back the bolt and trying the door. It opened at once.

The coldness of that first room hit me like a blow in the face. Architecturally it was the counterpart of Rose's sitting room, even the fireplaces were identical, but the effect was completely different. Rose's room was faded, sparsely elegant – very much her own style. This was burst plum plush, heavily upholstered, pelmeted and tasselled curtains, fringed and furry carpets, with sporting prints round the walls and magazines instead of books. There was a bureau near the window and several heavy little tables with bow legs, and a dark screen with oriental figures on it, golden pagodas, birds and flowers.

It was the screen that caught my full attention – because looking at it, I saw that the sections were canopied with cobwebs, and the spiders had long gone because the webs themselves were picked out with dust. Then I noticed that another web connected the white marble head to the tarnished brass fender, and it was dust that made a bloom on the plush – no one had sat in these chairs, or lit this fire for years and years, no one had opened these windows where the withered skeins of Virginia creeper clung unbroken. What stroke of doom had left the letter open on the bureau, the embroidery with the needle still piercing the cloth, the fragmented flower arrangement in a cut glass vase on the mantelpiece?

I don't know whether the piano was being played while I was looking round from my place just inside the door. Perhaps there had been a sympathetic or even dramatic pause in the music. But hearing it again, at once I noticed something odd about the sound. For I must be close to the instrument – closer at least than I had been in the hall – but it didn't seem any louder. Possibly Simon's foot had sunk on the soft pedal, but that didn't really explain the fact that the volume of the music was unchanged. It didn't sound as if it was in the next room. In a queer way it didn't sound as if it was anywhere. It had a *removed* quality.

47

All the same, when I crept across the plushy carpet to the door opposite, and putting the palm of my hand over the large cold white china knob, silently opened it, there was the piano, up on the right near the window. It was a heavy, old-fashioned grand, and Simon wasn't playing it. The pianist was a girl. She sat with her back to me, lazily, absent-mindedly following the tune. I saw her clearly because the creeper had been cleared from this window, so that it caught all the sun. She was wearing a pale-blue pleated skirt and a cream-coloured short-sleeved sweater, her arms were brown as if she'd just come back from holiday, and she had a gold watch on a gold linked bracelet on her left wrist, a gold wedding ring on that hand. There was an unusual formality about her clothes, and her attitude, and her flowery scent. Now I wouldn't have dreamt of saying hallo, unless she turned her head and saw me; but somehow I knew that she wouldn't. She was too absorbed in her tune and her thoughts. Besides, there was about her also this *removed* quality – almost as if I was watching her through a glass. But she was attractive even from the back, with her slim figure and springy, shoulder-length blonde hair.

I don't know how long I stood there watching and listening. But suddenly a door slammed in a distant part of the house, there was a rush and a scamper, and as I shrank hastily back into that morgue of a sitting room two dogs hurled themselves at me, leaping as high as my shoulders – skinny fawn dogs with spinal curvatures and crazy eyes – Mrs Wadham's whippets. At the same moment I heard her voice, thin, old, calling, 'Madman! Spectre!', her shuffling steps approaching down a flagged passage, more steadily than I liked, the intermittent thump of a stick. I pushed off the dogs and shut the door in their faces, flew across the sitting room and through the dividing door and bolted it behind me. I was trembling. It had very nearly been the worst way of meeting Rose's landlady.

But as I stood there with my hand still on the bolt, my breath coming hastily and jellified knees, I heard that further door, between the sitting and piano rooms, sharply open. Now I imagined her standing in the doorway, wearing her mohair stole, grasping her cripple's stick. And as I pressed my hot cheek against our door (which mercifully had a bolt, and a strong one), it vibrated under the onslaught of the dogs; they told the tale of the way I'd gone. So my terrified ears heard the shuffle-thump, shuffle-thump of her progress across the carpet; then there was a pause, but for dog snuffings under the door. Then – thump! thump! twice she struck upon the wooden panel next to my ear with her rubber-ended crutch, as if she could tell that I was very close, just the other side. And I dreaded that she would smash it in. But after another horrible pause, she shuffle-thumped away. I heard the inner door click shut behind her, and the yelp of one of the dogs as if, while manoeuvring, she trod on its foot.

After several cups of coffee in the by now positively tropical kitchen, I managed to bring my analytical expertise to bear on this episode. Whatever my reasons, I had trespassed and intruded, and Mrs Wadham had a right to be aggressive. As she had lived alone for years with no company or stimulation beyond her hyperactive dogs, her reaction was bound to be bizarre. If they told her there was danger, of course she felt threatened; for all she knew I was a burglar.

All the same, as the light left the little courtyard outside the kitchen window and the room began to darken, I didn't want to stay in the house. I thought I would call on Peter in his cottage, so leaving lights on in strategic places, I went out into the freezing afternoon. But as I was opening the top gate, I heard a modest poop and it was Rose, home early, so I got a lift back down the drive. I was glad I'd thought of turning off the oven before I left the house.

'But you didn't eat your lunch!' she exclaimed incredulously when she bent to check the fridge, which was always her first anxiety.

'I forgot.'

She shared the ham between us, and arranged a little salad. 'You're very odd about your meals, Christy,' she told me, seriously. 'You mustn't forget them. You could make yourself ill.'

But it cheered her evening, which might have been anxious otherwise, because she was wrapping up presents in very expensive paper, and needed to get the lengths just right, and the right kinds of messages on the cards.

'I've already done yours,' she said, in case I was worrying about it.

'Do you give anything to Mrs Wadham?'

'Oh no. I've already sent a card, through the post.'

'So really you never see each other.'

'It's not quite like that,' she said, looking at me across the beautifully patterned paper – medieval French it was. I had the impression that she wanted to spell out her relationship with her landlady, in order that I should understand another that was more intimate and important. 'We meet – but I've never been matey with anyone. I think it's a mistake.'

'But you can be friendly without being matey.'

'That's right, and then you're free to come and go. That's what I value.'

I felt a stab of pity for the fierce old woman next door. 'I'm glad she's got her family with her for Christmas,' I said.

Rose was cutting paper. She raised her head. 'What do you mean, family? She hasn't got any.'

'I don't know, I just imagined they were some sort of relations. There's a young man and a girl staying with her, anyhow.' Rose was looking completely bewildered. 'He's called Simon,' I added, in case that rang a bell.

'Are you sure, Christy? How do you know?'

'I saw him in the field yesterday, down by the stream.'

'I expect it was Peter from the farm.'

'No, I've met him, it wasn't. Anyway I heard Mrs Wadham calling him, that's how I know his name.'

Rose didn't believe me. 'I've never known her have visitors, not to stay, not in all the time I've been here.'

'Maybe they aren't staying. But no, they must be, Simon was in the garden last night, I saw him from my bedroom window. And I've heard the girl several times, playing the piano.'

'What do you mean, the piano!' Rose sounded positively outraged. 'It hasn't been touched for years, it's falling to pieces, even your brother couldn't get a note of music out of it!'

'Stuff!' I said rudely. 'It's a perfectly reasonable grand piano, and it isn't even out of tune!'

Rose put down the scissors and stared across the table at me, and her eyes were like steel pin points behind her specs. 'Have you been over there?'

'No,' I lied at once. 'I can tell it's reasonable, and in tune. When you hear as much music as I do, you know what you're listening to.'

'Christy,' said Rose, quietly and distinctly, 'I have been into Mrs Wadham's part of the house, and I have seen that piano. You are mistaken.'

'Then she's had it done up, for the young relations you don't believe she's got.'

Silence, but for the grinding of scissors through paper.

Rose said coolly, 'What does the girl look like?'

'Slim and blonde. I've only seen her from the back.'

Silence again, but for the snap of corners being mitred and stuck.

'I wonder if I ought to inform the police,' she said, speculatively.

'*Whatever for?*'

'I don't like the sound of it.'

'What harm can there possibly be? She knows the man.' That incident was clear, vividly clear in my mind. 'She's fond of him. I'd say she's known him a long time.' I stared across, hating Rose. 'Don't you think company might be good for her?'

Rose had stopped wrapping parcels, she was studying me. 'You're making it up,' she suddenly said.

Then I was furious with her, with her tiny mind, her petty ideas, her finicking way of carrying on, her idiotic assumption that 'informing the police' would solve everything. I said in the lightest and most flippant of my voices, the one that is like a red rag to Mother, 'Right, right! Look in tomorrow fans for the homeopathic brain surgeon and the Thing without a name! That's it for now. Good night all!' And I kicked back my chair, and slammed out.

U ntil that day, which was the 23rd, my diary is heavy with compulsive analysis of emotions, relationships etc. But that night I wrote only one sentence, 'Bloody angry with Rose.' And from then on, in what I might describe as the upward spiral of the rest of my stay, it consists of a kind of shorthand, disjointed and often violent – only excepting Christmas Day (not night) which stands out as something from another (yet another) world, really belonging to Rose.

She must have been worrying about me, because next morning she actually invited me to spend the day with her in the shop.

'No, thanks, I'd sooner stay here.'

'But, Christy! I can't possibly get back before five.'

'I don't care. I'm used to it.'

'Remember to have your lunch, anyway. Bacon and eggs, and I thought we'd have fish tonight –'

If I went with her to open the gates, it was only to see if there was a letter from Joel. Two for Rose, Christmas cards, feminine writing. One for Mrs Wadham, left in our box by mistake: Cynthia, she was called. And one – my heart lurched. I scuttled back to the house, didn't open it until I was safely shut in the kitchen, though he hadn't sealed it so I knew it was only a card, something impersonal that any sneak could pick up off the mantelpiece.

Heart pounding, hand trembling, mouth dry with excitement. J and an X – I pressed it to my lips in case he had. The picture was an abstract interpretation of the twelve days of Christmas in two colours, cheap run.

'Got any cards, Mum?'

'Have a look in the box. I think there's one or two left.'

What did I expect, the Wilton Diptych?

I stood the card on the table and made myself another cup of coffee. By the time I'd drunk it, I loved him as much as ever.

At this point I heard somebody walking down the passage.

I froze. The whole kitchen caught its breath, listening. The dripping tap had the beat of a frightened heart. A quick, light tread – the girl of course; fingers lightly brushing the panels of the kitchen door. I expected her to knock, but she didn't. The steps passed, went on up the stairs. I was standing by the table, gripping my cup. I put it down and missed the saucer. I replaced it very carefully with both hands.

I guessed at once what must have happened. The girl couldn't have been in the house for years, if Rose had never seen her. She hadn't realized that half of it was now let, and she'd walked in as a matter of course. How empty, how shabby all this would look to her! I washed up slowly, my ears tightly tuned to the passages and stairs, but nobody came. I polished the teaspoons – they were made of real silver – and put everything away.

It was a very cold, sparkling morning. The sunlight filtered through the laurels into the little courtyard outside the kitchen, shifted in kaleidoscopic patterns on the brittle window glass.

When there was nothing left to do I stood by the kitchen door for a while, awaiting developments. At last, as there weren't any, I opened it. The hall was full of light from the long window above. She was somewhere on the first floor – she must be. There was no second staircase. I took Joel's card and the envelope up to my room, arranged the card on

54

the table by my bed, pushed the envelope under my pillow. My movements were deliberate and slow. It wasn't that I was afraid of meeting her – not at all, I looked forward to that. But it was disconcerting not knowing quite how or when it would happen. Hide and seek is a jumpy game, even if you play it with your best friend.

I stood in the doorway of my room and stared down the empty, sunlit passage. The light was like summer, except that it was cold. I said, 'Hallo?' in a questioning sort of way. Nobody answered. Then I heard a noise, a tap-tapping, light and small. I thought it came from the big room at the end. If it was the girl, I didn't know what she could be doing there.

I began walking down the passage, paused halfway thinking the noise had stopped. And sure enough, all was silent. But soon it started again, and it did come from that room. And however much I wanted to meet that girl, my heart was beating fast high up in my throat within flapping distance of my mouth, dry not with love this time but apprehension. I stopped again just short of the doorway. The door was agape, I inched forward, looked through.

Nobody there. The room was empty and silent. But I detected a faint rose scent, as if she had looked in. Then I remembered the swallow and wondered whether it had only been frozen. If it had woken in the sun and was trying to get out, that would explain the tapping noise. So I walked across to the window, but no, it was dead, and had been a long time. Several butterflies had come to life though, and were now poised on different panes of sparkling glass. As I watched, on a shared and secret impulse they opened the dark velvety triangles of their wings and continued to beat with minute tappings against the panes, in their desire to reach the wintry garden. Their wing patterns, dull crimson, purple and pink, looked like jewels that needed cleaning.

LOVE LOVE LOVE between the butterflies, and I looked

down and saw Simon with one of the whippets, far below me in the field. He was staring up at the house. So I waved, but he didn't answer, and presently he turned and walked away towards the stream. Though he walked with a self-conscious straightness, like a soldier, he looked little and isolated against the line of trees. Perhaps it was that that made me sad – an idea of him as the Guardian of the Gate, Keeper of the Pass, Last Defender of the Flag. Or perhaps it was simply that word, LOVE: because the hand that wrote it was now old and the passion dust and ashes. I stood by the window thinking about Joel and me in a turgid, illogically miserable sort of way. It all meant so much in the present, and seemed to pass in a breath. Sad and sad I felt – adrift on a tide of melancholy – lost in a night without stars.

I was roused by an almighty crash. It came from Rose's bedroom, or mine – just the crash, then echoing silence. I ran out of the room and down the passage, threw open Rose's door, and saw at once what had happened. Her large wardrobe was lying face downwards on the floor. Behind it there was a door, papered over to match the rest of the room so that it wouldn't have showed if someone hadn't been through and broken the seal. The girl of the rose scent (of which a whiff still clung to the air) had escaped this way. This door was the double of the one downstairs that divided the two parts of the house; it would lead into the passage that had once connected all the upstairs rooms, which she would remember from long ago. She'd pushed the wardrobe to one side, and upset it. And I wasn't strong enough to heave it up by myself, so I would have to bear the lamentations of Rose.

I went quickly back to the kitchen. Everything I touched – the banister, the knob on the kitchen door, the things for making coffee – felt oddly warm, because my hands were so cold.

I sat at the table and wrote an illustrated letter to Dad, a fantasy on what was happening – Gothic house called Nightmare Abbey, vultures, spooks, Mrs Wadham on a broomstick, Rose in hysterics. I enjoyed doing it, made myself actually laugh aloud, finally stamped and addressed the envelope, and walked out to the letter box. There was no post for days, but he'd get it eventually. They'd all be in the middle of loading the car at this moment. Tempers would be frayed. Tim and Mum would be arguing about whether to take his trumpet – she likes him to give a recital to Granny & Co., and he hates it, he says it's hell playing to family, but it is her proudest hour and she always wins. I always stand up for him, but even so she was probably missing me in my usual role of extra person to remember essentials.

It was after two when I returned to the kitchen and I'd had nothing to eat since breakfast. I was about to start cooking when I noticed Mrs Wadham's letter propped up behind the taps. I'd meant to take it round earlier, assuming she didn't get much Christmas mail. So I got my jacket and went out again. I didn't know where to find her front door with, presumably, letterbox, but just then I heard the calves bellowing in the farmyard, and I guessed they were being fed. I walked that way, meaning to ask Peter what to do with the letter.

The glitter had gone with the morning, this afternoon was bleached and cruelly cold. The leaves of the evergreens rattled like dry bones as I pushed through. The red door had stiffened up in the frost, and by the time I got into the yard Peter had finished with the calves and gone. So I walked on between the buildings, taking the back way to his cottage, but as I was passing the harness room I caught a glimpse of him inside. I opened the door and went in, and was just in time to see his legs disappearing up the ladder into the loft.

I said, 'Peter!' It sounded a bit cheeky, but I didn't know his surname. 'I've got a letter here for Mrs Wadham – ' But he didn't answer, or look down. He didn't move, either; the loft was strangely silent. I put the letter, which I was carrying, into my pocket, crossed the room, started after him up the ladder. It stood straight up, fastened against the wall. The roughly made rungs were too far apart for comfort.

But the coldness, as I mounted the third rung – as if the loft was packed with snow! 'Peter?' I said. I tipped back my head and stared into the square opening at the top of the ladder. And in that black hole there hung a face, that seemed to come together gradually as my eyes adjusted to the darkness, as if it was being painted in from behind by an invisible brush held in an invisible hand. And the eyes, staring down into mine — the brilliant, wicked eyes – they were not Peter's.

I missed the lower rungs and fell in a heap, and scrambled out of that little cold room as if he was floods or fire. I was terrified he'd come after me; at the corner I cast a hasty, backward glance, but nobody appeared. I hurried on, tripping and gasping. It wasn't until I was in sight of the cottage that it occurred to me that the man might belong on the farm. Maybe that derelict place supported two workers; it seemed unlikely, but it was possible. I stopped some minutes at Peter's gate, trying to calm down. I knew how sharp his eyes were, and I didn't want to look a complete fool.

The neatness of his garden was somehow comforting. Even the dead chrysanthemums were staked. A short paved path led round to the front door, on which I knocked, and he opened it himself. I could have hugged him, I was so glad he was in, though the rest of his family were in town shopping for Christmas. He talked about them while he fetched an extra cup for the tray of tea waiting in the front room, where there were Christmas decorations and a diagonal flight of plaster ducks, and a very fat, grizzled collie lying in front of the fire, who opened one eye at me and thumped her tail.

I drank several cups of tea and ate most of a plate of fairy cakes and gradually, in the civilized warmth of his cottage, I got back my sense of proportion. For this had really frightened me – what if Rose had been right after all? What if the people I'd seen – the man in the loft made three – were criminals, about to rob Mrs Wadham? But now I could see that as usual, I'd been exaggerating things. The girl at the piano couldn't be a crook, neither could Simon. If the man in the loft was one – and he did look like one – that was in no way my problem.

So I said, changing the subject more abruptly than was polite, 'Do you have any help on the farm?'

'Not any more. Back along, there was half a dozen men on this place, not counting the extra hands taken on for the hay harvest and the corn, but that's looking right back, 'tis only myself now, for the store cattle.'

'I wondered, because I saw somebody out there. I thought it was you, but it wasn't.'

His expression sharpened. 'When was this to?'

I told him. 'What do you think he was up to?'

'Just looking about I daresay, on the chance of something worth picking up. We don't want none of those visitors. I'll chase after him presently, when you've finished your tea.'

There was only one picture in the room, an enlarged photograph elaborately mounted and framed. Mown lawns and clipped hedges, the house almost covered with creeper, more of the sentry box visible over the cropped tops of the yews. 'That's Wadham's,' Peter said, nodding towards it. 'The old place hasn't looked like that for a year or two, nor never will again in my opinion. Captain Wadham snapped it, last time he come home on leave; lucky he did; 'twere the last photograph ever he took, poor man.'

He got up to peer at it with a queer sort of respect, even a reverence for much more than a beautiful house.

'Back in 1940 that was took, and I'd been working on the place a twelvemonth; fourteen, that's all I was, but I remember it clear as yesterday. We'd a dry spell never known before or since, and the creeper come on early the colour of blood, like in memory of dead fighting men. Even the stream ran dry that year, they did say it was some earth tremor or that, like deep underground, did it, more than what you might call a drought. We'd to water the horses out of the yard, from the well in under, five riding horses the Captain kept, and Mrs Wadham she liked to ride. It made you proud to see them out together. Looking at that picture I always think 'tis a pity there wasn't the colour photographs then like there is today, it was that pretty with the green grass and the house all over scarlet. . . . So the Captain went back to London on the afternoon train as I know for 'twas my father drove him to the station. We never saw him again.' He paused, to prolong the drama of it.

'Next morning he was dead, killed in a air raid. 'Twere Mrs Wadham gave Dad that picture. Just handed it to him Christmas time without a word. She tried to persuade the Captain not to go, stay another night she said, I can hear her to this very hour. But he wouldn't stay. She had a preposition that's what she had but she couldn't persuade him. Poor woman, she didn't go riding no more.'

He went into the kitchen and put on his coat and boots, and we went out. The sky was colourless, ugly, opaque. I asked, 'Will it snow?'

'Not unless the wind goes round to the northwards. That's where our snow comes from.'

My heart beat faster as we approached the harness room. Peter went in and climbed the ladder while I watched through the window. I don't know what I expected to happen but I was ready to run. But he came down again at once, shut the door and locked it, and put the key in his pocket. He said, 'He's gone now, at any rate.'

'Did he take anything?'

'What would he take? There's nothing, only calves, and he couldn't get through with a lorry up the track. Did he look like a thief?'

'Maybe he did, a bit. I'll draw him for you, if you like.' I know what made me offer to do it – I wanted him to say, 'Oh yes, that's old Bob (or Bill or Tom) from the village, he's often up here. I'll see him later on in the pub and ask him what he wants.' With all my heart I was wishing there to be a safe, ordinary reason for the appearance of that man.

I found paper and a pen in my pocket and did a quick sketch of the face, all I had seen of it – but it was like, it was an exact likeness. And I showed it to Peter. There was an odd little silence, while he looked at it. Then he asked, still studying the sketch, 'Was this an old man?'

'Oh no – about thirty or so. Maybe not that.'

He glanced at me then, and shook his head. At once I saw that he was displeased for some reason, but he only said, 'I should keep out of there, if I was you.' He turned his back and walked off.

I said after him, 'Thanks for the tea.'

'No trouble. I'll be seeing you.' But he sounded grumpy. As he was going round the corner I thought of calling, 'Happy Christmas!' Perhaps he didn't hear. He didn't answer.

Then I realized that the paper I'd pulled out to draw on was Mrs Wadham's letter, totally forgotten by me. There on the back leered the face – in felt pen, so there it had to stay. Silly of me, and had I been able to foresee the consequences of this error, I might have dropped it straight into the bin, even if it was 'interfering with Her Majesty's mails'.

I got over the fence and walked along the front of the house, the way I'd gone before. I seemed to remember a door there, and soon I discovered it, a deep-set, cobwebby, creeper-covered door which had a bell as well as a letter box. I pushed the letter in, and pulled out the bell – it was on a spring – and seconds later, in the stony heart of the house, I heard it faintly jangle. Then I bolted. But her dogs caught up with me as, with an idiotically hammering heart, I was scrambling back into the farm. They weren't vicious, only pleased at this interruption in their existence. They were instantly obedient to the thin wail from their mistress, 'Madman – Spectre – Here, dogs!'

I looked back. She was standing out in the cold, staring after me; tall, bony as a witch, still wearing the scarlet stole, as if she never took it off; holding the letter in one hand she stooped slightly upon the crutch grasped in the other.

It was getting dark, and I had noticed before that there was something mysterious about entering the empty old house in the evening. One had a definite feeling of company, not exactly a crowd, but lingering in the shadows the almost visible imprints of people who had lived out their lives there, and who dispersed, one after another, as the lights went on. It wasn't too much of an unpleasant, or frightening feeling. But it made me cautious. I certainly wouldn't have gone into the cupboard for a suitcase, not after dark.

Rose came back soon, and I had to tell her about the wardrobe. The news immediately threw her into a flap. She couldn't believe that it had fallen on its own, and of course it hadn't, but I knew better than to mention the girl. We trudged upstairs to her bedroom. I knew she thought I'd been snooping. We examined the collapsed piece of furniture as well as we could without lifting it.

'Things do fall,' I said. It sounded ridiculous. Rose looked crossly across at me. We took opposite sides and heaved. The thing was horribly heavy.

'Did you know there was a door there?' I pointed to the

papered outline revealed by the crash. Now I noticed a key sticking out of it – which struck me as odd.

'Yes – no – I don't remember. Do help, Christy. I can't possibly move this on my own!'

'I'll just make sure it's locked. You don't want people – I mean, anyone could get in from next door.'

I twisted the key to lock the door. To my astonishment, it was locked already.

'Do help! What's the matter? You look as if you've seen a ghost! Oh dear, oh dear, I suppose this it too much for you, I shall have to get Peter over, and that's asking favours, that's something I never do. No, leave it alone, you mustn't strain yourself.'

'It's okay, for God's sake!' I almost shrieked. I felt as if she was plucking out my nerves. It had just occurred to me that *the girl might be inside the wardrobe*. We struggled together; inch by inch we managed to lever it up. 'It's oak, you see,' panted Rose. 'Really I don't understand how it could have fallen. It isn't wormy. The legs are perfectly sound.' I understood, all too well. At last we had it upright. I held my breath while she opened the door. I expected a body to slump out, unconscious – dead even. 'Oh dear, oh dear,' she was bleating, automatically. I peered round. Her soft, heather-coloured clothes heaped the bottom of the cupboard. She began lifting them, putting them back on hangers. I waited breathlessly for an arm or a leg to be uncovered. Nothing. Clothes, and clothes only (many more than I would have expected) had fallen with the wardrobe.

Supper was boil-in-a-bag, nice and tasty. I worked out that the girl, having knocked over the wardrobe while trying to get at the door, had crept out while I was shut in the kitchen, writing to Dad. Evidently she didn't share my desire for a meeting and conversation.

Rose had some washing to do, and a skirt to iron. These chores filled her entire evening. I read.

63

'I do hope you aren't feeling sad, Christy?' she asked. She had been pondering over possible reasons for my unsociable behaviour.

'Why should I be?'

Then I remembered that it was Christmas Eve, which used to be my favourite night of the year. And it would have been sad if the others had been hanging up their stockings, but we'd given that up years ago.

That night between Christmas Eve and Christmas Day, I floated so to speak in the shallows of sleep. If there'd been the slightest disturbance I'd have woken immediately, but there wasn't, not so much as the dripping of a tap, because our plumbing had frozen solid. Only one pipe, down in the kitchen, now flowed. I was amazed by Rose's calmness. I imagined my mother's fury, if the same thing had happened at home: she would have had the plumber out by the ears, Christmas or no Christmas.

So this was on my mind, with the events of the day before, and as a result I dreamt a lot. I dreamt of icebergs in the shapes of wardrobes. I dreamt of gallons and gallons of water, very dark and cold, filling the loft over my head, all ready to burst through the ceiling. I dreamt that there was a flood upstairs, and I ran down, but Peter's dog was snarling in the hall and I couldn't get past. And each time, before my kayak was crushed or I was drowned or devoured, I surfaced neatly. It is a knack I learnt early in life, for I have always had an active sleep. But oh, this was a house for dreams! Never in my life had I dreamt so much, and never will again.

The last of them was very strange in that I was so barely asleep, it didn't feel like a dream at all. I dreamt I was walking up the strip of lawn towards the summerhouse at the end of the garden. It was a hot afternoon, thundery and oppressive. The smell of roses, caught between the wall and the hedge, was really too sweet for pleasure. Several small dark birds were wheeling and swooping over the lawn;

swallows, I thought, flying low which means that it is going to rain. And still I was walking over the grass, and it seemed to take a long time, as if the garden had grown much bigger, or I had shrunk.

Then it came to me that I was following someone, and a panicky pulse started beating in my chest. I knew that the person would be inside the summerhouse, so when I reached it, I didn't climb the steps, but I looked through the open door. The girl I had seen playing the piano was standing inside with her back to me. I had an instant, hideous knowledge of impending disaster. I moved quickly to warn her, but at the same moment she turned and rapidly began to climb the wooden staircase that led through a square opening to the first floor. And I caught a glimpse of her face. It was beautiful. She was radiantly, passionately in love.

I knew who was up there waiting for her, without a shadow of doubt I knew. I tried to call her back, but my throat tightened as if I was being strangled. Then anything I could utter was drowned in the storm that suddenly broke outside. I was impaled by lightning – drenched – deafened by the thunder pounding on the roof of the summerhouse—

Rose knocking on the door, switching on the light. I struggled awake to her diffident summons. 'Christy? Happy Christmas! We'll have to leave in about an hour.'

I lay for a while, recovering. My nightclothes were soaked with sweat. Then I crept down to the misery of a cold wash under the kitchen tap. She came in as I was finishing. Maybe it was the challenge of the freeze, maybe it was the thought of seeing The Friend that made her cheeks glow. She looked positively pretty that Christmas morning.

'How long will this go on?' I growled.

'I don't know. I missed the forecast.'

'But I *need* baths! I *like* them!'

'Oh dear, but I expect it'll thaw soon.'

66

We humped buckets of water up to the loo. It was degrading.

Rose cut out the breakfast toast because she said we were going to have such a super lunch. Apparently The Friend was a super cook. She mentioned his name: Huntley. Would I mind wearing a skirt, because Huntley was hopelessly old-fashioned and really liked girls to look like girls, and she did want us to get on well together. I didn't mind – I liked my skirt. It was emerald green and royal blue and woolly, and I wore a huge jersey with an Indian top underneath in case Huntley's place was heated. We were ready hours too soon for a lunch date, but Rose suggested going to church on the way. I knew that had been her intention all along, that was why she'd woken me so early, but in the circumstances I was grateful.

We loaded the little car with presents, including two bottles of champagne as our contribution to the lunch. Rose was in a state of high fuss, and I felt jollier than I'd expected. It was good to get out for the day, even if it did involve a church service, and anyway that gave me an excuse to wear my hat. It was black felt, ex-Covent Garden prop cupboard ('Coppelia' was printed on a label inside) and I had managed to fit the whole of my badge collection on the crown, from 'Have a Good Day' to 'Blood Donor' with a picture of a bat. Rose looked sideways at it once or twice, but she had won the great Battle of the Skirt (as she thought) so she said nothing.

At home we don't go to church, except for weddings, or to hear Tim in a concert. Granny calls herself 'practising', whatever that may mean, and this church, in the centre of the town, was what she would have termed 'high'. It had holy water in a basin by the door – Rose crossed herself – and a light by the altar to which she genuflected. It was pretty full, including several loud babies.

I sat and thought about Joel. I'd rather neglected him

67

over the past twenty-four hours, what with one thing and another, and it was a luxury to let my love-inflamed imagination play over him in slow motion. He couldn't afford to spend much on clothes and he wore jeans mostly, with Oxfam sweaters and jackets in ugly colours. I dressed him in brown and gold to match his skin and hair, I gave him Italian shoes and a leather jacket. I was married in the same sort of colours, styled slimmingly; I'd trimmed my own hat. Mum looked nice, and now it was happening, she was making the best of it; Dad was cool and collected at my elbow. Joel's mother, who looks like a bus and always wears bright red at school functions, filled the front pews with the rest of his family. Tim played us fanfares from the organ loft, gladdening, goldening the ceremony. The reception was a bit stiff but soon we went away to an incredibly plush hotel booked for us by Dad, and we got into bed immediately. Happy thoughts! Though I knew that wild horses wouldn't drag Joel up an aisle, it would be the registry office for us, if it happened.

Meanwhile the vicar was intoning in his floating gold, clouded with incense. A woman sang a solo, and very good she was, clean and cold as a blade. She made me wish that someone had thought of giving me religion. It must be a comfort to be able to send messages Out There, reply assured if you do the right things. Too late – I'd missed the Heavenly Bus; but Rose hadn't, she was a secure passenger, to judge from her expression. She stayed on her knees in prayer for several minutes after the service was over, and I sat beside her, holding my hat and wishing I could read her thoughts. What did she want from God? Hypermarkets for the Third World? Huntley at the altar? If it was him, her passion was under control. You couldn't have told from her pale, composed countenance and eyes downcast behind the specs that sex lurked under the camisole.

I remembered my dream. That was my sort of sex – the

blood pounding in the heart, the legs melted to water still carrying me quickly upstairs. While I was thinking about it, Rose opened her eyes and turned to me a little surprised, as though her meditations had momentarily obliterated my existence. She collected her prayer book, handbag and gloves, and we went out. The crowd had dispersed by this time. The sky was cold blue glass with a distant radiance, as though God was celebrating Christmas far away in Heaven. And from another church started a clamour of bells, as though they had got loose and were leaping about in the tower.

Nothing of 'I run, I run, I am gathered to thy heart' with Rose. She drove soberly to Huntley's house, which was the last in a perfectly preserved Georgian terrace, conveniently close to the town centre yet secluded from most of the traffic. Mother would approve of this, I thought, getting out of the car and sizing up the property: this is what she would call a gem. The front door opened and Huntley appeared, dressed exactly as I expected in a buttoned cardigan with expensive silk scarf tucked in round the neck – a present from Rose? – corduroy trousers, and leather slippers. I studied him across the strip of garden. Smallish brown eyes, on the hot side; receding crimped brown hair; skin a bit rough and reddish, as if he'd had problems in his youth but was now into the right diet; nose a thought squashy. And Rose looked round with her hair fluffed out, her specs clinging to her nostrils, her cheeks pink with incipient fluster. Suddenly sweet Rose! Ah, 'tis love, 'tis love, etc. I hauled out Mum's mammoth parcel, which for some reason was coming untied, and clamping the bottles under one arm, walked up the weedless paved path, Rose following with the rest. Huntley then darted down the steps to relieve me of the drink, in case I made the mistake of trying to shake his hand. And we went into the house.

I was very hungry, and a tantalizing smell filtered from

the kitchen down the striped wall-papered passage, distracting for the time my habit of observation, though later I noted the perfection of Huntley's habitat. Not a thing could I spot that was in bad taste anyway – discounting of course my coat, of the dark and hairy variety, left by me in a heap at the bottom of the stairs and speedily tidied into a cupboard with Rose's boots, too wide at the top for her legs, while she nudged her bony feet into embroidered mules. Then we were ushered into the pale-yellow and oyster striped drawing-room with its signed prints and gas log fire that flamed in toning colours of apricot, pink and yellow. Mother would have settled down here – taken the best armchair (none of them looked specially comfortable), drunk several glasses of sherry, eaten more than her share of turkey. No messing with Mother – 'Why doesn't he marry you, Rose, if you think so much of each other?' For the first time in months I really wished she was there, while I sipped from my cold yellow glass. Yes, I prefer my sherry sweetish and warmish, and I like to be given full measure. But Rose had done her protesting bit while he was pouring it, and I suppose he thought I wanted the same amount. I noticed he topped his up to the brim however.

It turned out that Rose had given Huntley a signed print, which pleased him, but now he was in a quandary about how to frame it. Ought it to be mounted, what did I think? The trend was to do without mounts; however with such a delicately tinted picture (yellow, pink and oyster – well played Rose) perhaps a mount was necessary to set it off. Of course it would have to be glazed; should it be a narrow black frame, or a perfectly plain narrow gilt one – what did Rose think? Or might one cleverly catch the colours within the gold? What he meant was one of those frames made of gilded wood that somehow picked up the main tones of the picture, did we know what he meant? So they discussed it, while I had long finished my sherry and was sniffing the aromas of the lunch, hoping Huntley hadn't forgotten anything, and wondering why, if we couldn't eat, we shouldn't at least open some of the parcels arranged tantalizingly round the miniature tree decorated only with silver icicles and ornaments of clear glass.

The dining room, when at last we got into it, was papered with maroon and oyster stripes, the maroon bits furry to the touch. The curtains were silk, and oyster-coloured. (There was a lot of oyster about Huntley.) The Regency table with its sparkling silver and glass, and narrow red streamers arranged diagonally instead of mats, on which were marshalled the salt and pepper, bread sauce, stuffing in individual balls, gravy and cranberry sauce, contributed to the gourmet flavour of the exquisite turkey, glazed carrots, buttery baby sprouts and feathery potatoes. Huntley popped open the champagne and I drank several foaming glasses, and ate more than was polite, but it was such a controlled feast, I was afraid there wouldn't be enough; while Rose and Huntley toyed with the glory of it, and talked about how odd it was that people nearly always got the lampshades wrong.

But as the champagne worked upon my eager spirits, I noticed more and more Rose's delicate pleasure and pale excitement; I could see that in her way she loved Huntley madly. I managed to clear away the turkey plates without a disaster, and then it was the plum pudding clothed in blue flame and the iced syllabub, and the second bottle of champagne. At this point he pushed towards Rose a tiny, beautifully wrapped box. I was watching her face and I thought my God, if this is a jumping bean or other joke I shall prong old Huntley with my dessert fork. 'What can this be?' she wondered in an unnatural voice, and 'Open it now!' he urged. So she did, gently untying and unfolding with her thin, vulnerable fingers, and it wasn't a ring, and I could feel in my own heart her snatch of disappointment.

71

But it was very nice, a locket; and then there was more careful chat about what to put in it, and he fastened it round her neck, and I told her how pretty it looked.

After the lunch I cleared all away on the wobbly trolley, and installed myself in the kitchen to do the washing-up. Huntley put his arms round me as I stood at the sink, which I had more or less expected, because he had drunk even more than I had and Rose was safely enthroned in the sitting room. I didn't respond, and he muttered something like 'Lovely girl' into my hair and then made coffee in a complicated gadget. There was a tv in the kitchen, so I finished the dishes and settled down in front of it with a mug of Nescaff. I sat through two old films and hoped they were getting down to brass tacks next door.

At dusk I made tea. I could only find China, but I put in a lot, and carried it through on a tray with mugs. They were still in their chairs with the fireplace between them, but they hadn't turned on the lights which was a hopeful sign. My tea wasn't Huntley's style, and he had a glass of port while we opened our presents. It took a long time because after each opening the paper had to be folded and the string coiled; there was none of the scrabbling and ripping that goes on at home. Tim gave me tapes of my favourite groups recorded by himself, much appreciated by me because what with his deadly practising and schoolwork, he hasn't much free time. Dad sent books, chosen as he explained for the pictures: Jane Austen, Mervyn Peake, a beautiful Hans Andersen. Mum sent sweets, chocolates and clothes, all good.

So all in all I'd had an excellent Christmas. And Rose was very pleased with her things. And now it was time to go back to Wadhams. I went ahead down the path, giggling to myself and dropping things, keeping my back turned so I can't say whether they kissed. We left Huntley in a farewell attitude on the steps.

At first neither of us spoke. The town was almost deserted. The Christmas decorations in the centre looked like a failed party; public jollity is difficult to achieve in England, people don't like it, and expect it to rain. But tonight was clear, above the hideous loom of the street lights; clear, and colder than ever. I remembered there would be no baths for us, and my spirits took a downward turn. I said, 'I wish we'd thought of having baths at Huntley's.'

'Oh no,' said Rose at once. 'We couldn't have done that. Anyway we'd have had to get home afterwards, we'd have caught our deaths.'

There was a pause while she negotiated a mini-roundabout, slowing down and signalling though there was nothing else about. Then she remarked, self-consciously, 'It was nice that you came.'

'I enjoyed it.' That sounded inadequate. 'I liked meeting Huntley.'

'He's rather a special sort of person.'

'He's a great cook. Does he always feed you as well as that?'

'Oh no! He eats very simply as a rule, toast and pâté perhaps with a glass of wine. He makes his own pâté. And soup – he never uses packets or tins.'

We progressed for a while in silence. But I had the feeling that Rose was about to take a plunge, and I was right.

'It was nice of you to wash up,' she said presently. 'You didn't –' here she brushed nervously at a wisp of hair – 'you didn't leave us alone on purpose, did you?'

'I wanted to watch the telly.'

'That's what I thought. That's what I told Huntley. You weren't bored?'

'Not a bit.'

'Oh good. It's just that we would have felt very awkward if you had felt awkward about coming in to sit with us.'

'Of course not!'

'Because we wouldn't have minded. You see we feel it's not sensible, at our age, to rush into things.'

By now we were out of the town, and the car was nosing its way between hedges, the frosty road glittering ahead down the white shaft of the headlamps. All round the country was dark, black dark, as only open country can be.

'What I mean is, if it happens – you know what I mean, if Huntley does decide to adapt his way of life, to include me I mean – '

'I think it would be a very good thing.'

'Oh do you really, Christy? I *am* glad to hear you say that! Of course I feel – in other words I've felt for some time that it *might* be right, but it's so difficult to know when you're personally involved. I *am* glad – you mean you think it might be a good thing if things worked out for us, together I mean?'

'I'm sure it would. I think you're very well-suited. I'm sure Mum would think so.'

'Well, yes, but then I rather particularly haven't talked about any of this to Susan, you know how she jumps to conclusions.'

'That's okay, I won't mention it.'

'Well, I knew you wouldn't.' A pause. 'Did it strike you – could you see that Huntley's rather – fond of me? I mean, did it show?'

'Yes, of course. He gave you a beautiful present.'

'I'm pleased. He must have chosen it with care.'

I couldn't imagine Huntley choosing even a bag of sugar without care, he was the antithesis of an impulse buyer. I got out to open the gate. Stupidly I had difficulty with the catch, it was the champagne perhaps. Caught in the headlights, the black yew bushes looked like people waiting

74

for us, muffled up in cloaks. 'Can you manage?' cried Rose within the sealed box of her car.

'Yes, I've got it!' And I swung it open, and she drove through.

While we were drinking our bedtime cocoa, she suddenly said, 'I've been thinking what to put in my locket.'

'What?'

'I wondered, could you paint me a miniature of Huntley? I can lend you a snapshot to copy.'

'Sure! I'd like to.'

Later still I barged into the kitchen without thinking of knocking, and surprised Rose washing at the sink. She was naked to the waist, very slim, white, virginal – unmarred by sex or age. And all this was his if he liked. Profound physiological as well as psychological questions: why had she waited all these years for what in the end turned out to be Huntley? What made her love *him*? It was a mystery, but her hopefulness, her humility that was not feeble but strong, touched me in my heart. (Dad may argue that the heart is an organ, a pumping machine; all I can say is, the keenest feelings tell me exactly where mine lies in my chest.) Add all this to Christmas church in the morning, and it explains why I went upstairs without waiting for my turn at the sink, and knelt (with a degree of embarrassment, but going by pictures that was how people did it) beside my bed, and asked God (if there was One) to unite Rose and Huntley. The prayer was a bit sticky at first, but I worked at it. After all, I knew what it was to love and to suffer, and for me there was plenty of time.

Afterwards I piled on the sweaters and got into bed. I intended to write up my diary, but I was trapped by one of my Christmas books and read for a long time. Reading never makes me sleepy, and by the time I put it down because of an overpowering, champagne-induced thirst, my mind felt hyperactive although it was after midnight. I opened my door quietly and stepped out into the passage. All was still, Rose rapt, wrapped in sleep. I fetched my towel and toothbrush and went silently downstairs.

I'd turned on the landing light, but there was no upstairs switch for the hall. Even so the ground floor was not of course completely dark, and the banisters particularly seemed to catch the low-powered radiance filtered from above, as though years of polish had given them a luminosity which, extinguished by day, still glowed at night. In other words they looked exciting, like stairs down to a ball. I was still thinking about the book I had been reading, and really Christmas altogether had been much nicer than I expected.

I had just reached the hall when I heard the piano next door – at this hour for goodness' sake! Nothing new – no whirl of Brahms or Beethoven – not even Carols for Everyone including guitar chords and plum pudding recipe. No, it was just the same sleepy Cole Porter melodies, carelessly, languidly played. Without stopping to think about it I crossed the hall and put my hand on the door. I was dressed in pyjamas and three huge jerseys and I hadn't washed, or brushed my hair, but suddenly there seemed no

76

valid reason why I shouldn't hide in Mrs Wadham's unused sitting room to listen to these last echoes of her Christmas. No light showed under the door. I could safely assume that that first room was empty.

It wasn't. A young man was standing by the window. He was reading a letter, and as I came in he raised his head and I saw that it was Simon. He looked straight at me, but as I opened my mouth to blurt out some excuse, he simply returned to his letter. Apparently he was so deep in it, he hadn't seen me there.

And now I realized that I must be asleep, in one of those exhausted but brilliant dreams I seemed recently to be specializing in. For this was a summer afternoon. The sun was streaming in through the open window, and a breath of warm wind moved the thin letter paper, carried in a scent of roses and hay. (Roses and hay, at Christmas! Definitely I was asleep, and so invisible to Simon.) Then the room, though identically furnished, was different somehow – brighter. On the mantelpiece, crowning the marble head with flowers, stood a vase of coloured daisies and what Mum calls 'jip'. A newspaper lay on the table, a white lacy jacket hung over the screen. The bureau was open, as though Simon had only just got up from the chair which was pushed back against the brass fender. And the windows were very clean, the furniture dusted, the brass polished to pale gold.

The music stopped in the next room, between one bar and the next. The girl spoke. 'Simon?'

'Yes,' he said, without looking up.

'I just wondered if you were still there.'

And the music began again, a different tune.

Then I caught my breath in this trance of mine, in this dream. A dog, a fawn whippet, very like Mrs Wadham's but smaller and older, with white hairs in its muzzle, came out from behind the sofa and trotted across the room towards me. It behaved as if it could see me. As I shrank from it, it veered away, bounded towards Simon and gently laid its nose against his free hand. He muttered, 'Phantom – good girl.' Then he roused himself, looked out of the window, stuffed the letter into his pocket. He said, 'I'm going to give the dog a walk. Coming?'

'No, it's too hot,' she answered, over the tune she was playing.

He didn't try to persuade her. He said, 'Come on then,' to the dog, and they went out through the door where I was standing – empty air to Simon; indeed the whole world was empty air to him, to judge from his expression. All I felt was a shiver as he passed, the sort they say is a goose walking over your grave.

The music continued for a while. Then it stopped again. The girl in the next room said, 'Are you still there?'

Then there was silence, a silence that for some reason became ominous. And now in my chest the pulse started that was going to swell into a panic; I began to be afraid, yes very afraid, without knowing why. The breeze had dropped, the room was caught in summer stillness; she was right, it was too hot, and the smell of flowers was too much, like a perfumery department. But I had the crazy feeling that somebody had been waiting for Simon to go, and now this person had come in through the door just behind me, our own dividing door. I had the insane idea that I was about to feel his arms round me, and I was terrified, too terrified to turn or move except for my eyes which stared down at my hands gripping my towel and toothbrush – what a parcel of reality to carry into a dream!

There was a crash in the next room as the girl jumped up from the piano, knocking over the stool. Next moment she appeared in the doorway. Her blue eyes were wide open and her lips parted, as she looked straight through me. She had been waiting too – for him. She walked quickly round the sofa to the window, and from behind me, through me, after her was drawn a shivering darkness, to a dark outline, to a broad-shouldered man in shirt, breeches, scuffed leather shoes, neither gentlemanly or clean, but powerful, purposeful, predatory. His presence so filled her senses that she only just remembered to step away from the window where someone might catch sight of her; she raised her right hand, as if to hold him off, but it was a trembling, ineffectual gesture. I knew that it made him smile, though I couldn't see his face. I knew who he was. What I didn't know was what I was going to do if there was no way out, as I groped frantically behind me for the handle and wrenched open the door.

And there lay the incredibly comforting, empty hall with the uncarpeted stairs and wan light on the landing. I slammed the door shut – then stopped, still grasping the handle that seemed to divide sleeping and waking. I couldn't understand what had happened. Surely I had been dreaming? Was I still asleep?

I put my ear to the wooden panel, heard nothing. I thought for a minute. Then, sleeping or waking, I dreamed or walked myself upstairs and into bed, and knew no more until late next morning.

There was a note on the kitchen table. 'Didn't like to wake you. Back later p.m., food in fridge. Snap in envelope if you feel like doing a picture. Love –' yes! Love! – 'R'.

I opened the envelope: close-up of Huntley naked to the waist, looking coy but confident. Beach in background, strong light – souvenir probably of the Italian trip. I made some coffee and couldn't stop yawning. I washed up out of the kettle, and burnt my fingers. All the time I was listening; at last I went and stood by the dividing door. It seemed to me that the piano must start again, or the voices, but I don't know what I would have done if I had heard anything. Probably at that stage I wouldn't have risked another eavesdropping. I felt the shell of myself – drained out.

Then the doorbell rang, whirring like an electric shock in the silence and the emptiness, making me jump. I spun round and scuttled upstairs, because the bathroom window overlooked the courtyard, and I thought I'd make sure who was there before I opened the door.

Joel.

My heart skidded out of its usual pattern. He was wearing his donkey jacket, jeans, scarf and new lace-up boots. He was staring around with a mixture of amusement and impatience, as if he'd never seen such a crazy set-up, as if he didn't expect to have to wait for doors, especially girls' doors, to open. I hadn't time to brush my hair or change into something more flattering. I tried to open the window but it wouldn't because, I now saw, Rose had painstakingly sticky-taped it all round. But he heard and looked up. I waved and went down. My heart was thudding.

I opened the door. He was still standing in the middle of the yard with uplifted profile, and I noticed that he'd unwound the scarf one turn. He has a theatrical streak which can be irritating, but then he looks like an actor with a glamour that makes me weak at the knees. And here it all was on my doorstep; it was only a pity that I wasn't looking my best. 'Hi,' I said. 'I wasn't expecting you,' and I remembered that particular letter I'd written, and felt myself starting to blush.

He looked round. 'What's this?' he said. 'The Moated Grange or what?'

'We don't live in all of it.' Then I wished I hadn't said that. It sounded as though I was trying to excuse the grandeur of the place. Rose could be grand – why not?

'I thought they were keeping you prisoner!'

'Come in.'

'Is it safe? Where's the witch?'

I'd forgotten that joke between us. 'She's gone out.'

'Good timing!'

As he was passing me in the doorway he stopped and looked down and said, 'How are you, anyway?' and kissed me quickly on the lips, and then he stopped again in the passage and stared about and said, 'God! What a ruin!' I directed him on into the kitchen and there I put the kettle on again, mostly keeping my back turned. I was glad I'd done the washing-up; it looked squalid enough with flannels and toothbrushes lying on the sink.

'Is this where you had Christmas?'

'No, we went out, to a friend. It was good, I enjoyed it. How did you get here?'

'I had a lift down. There's a party, they asked me to go and I said I wouldn't, and then I remembered you were near so I changed my mind. You're invited.'

'Okay, thanks.' But I was sharply, disconcertingly

conscious of not much wanting to go. Though I was trembling with excitement, the spoon of coffee jigging over the cup – which he noticed, he was quick to spot that sort of clue.

'If that's for me, I don't want it.'

I switched off the kettle. He moved up behind me and put his hands on my arms. 'You're lovely, Christy,' he said huskily into my hair. Huntley's image flicked across my mind. 'It's been a long time. Too long. How long is it? Six whole days?' Everything he said sounded as if he had lifted it from a soap opera. Why had this never struck me before? He moved his hands forward to my chest. I looked down on his fingers feeling about, they were brown even in winter. 'Why are you wearing so many sweaters?' he complained.

'It's cold here. Would you sooner have tea? I'm afraid there isn't anything else.'

'No, we had a beer on the way down. God I've missed you, Christy.'

'I've missed you as well.' But it sounded stilted. I felt stupidly awkward, and couldn't understand myself. Hadn't I been longing for this?

His hand got too bold, and I jerked away. 'Stop messing about,' I snapped.

'What's wrong?' I couldn't answer, I didn't know. 'Where's your room?' he said, after a bit. 'Or do you have to sleep under the table?'

'Don't be stupid!'

'Come on then, we've got time. Ed won't be back for an hour.'

(Ed: 'How long do you want? It's bloody cold for hanging about.' Joel: 'Come back in an hour – that'll be time enough.' Ed: 'Okay. I hope she'll be worth the mileage!')

Joel was squeezing me. 'Come on, Christy, be a good girl! It's a long way. I was thinking about you all the way down.'

(Joel: 'What about a quick one?' Ed: 'I thought you had this girl waiting for you.' Joel, with a laugh, running fingers through hair in typical soap-opera gesture: 'She'll wait!')

I said, 'Sorry. I don't want to.'

A brief blank silence. Then, 'You can't expect me to believe that. I got your letter.' Knead, press. Hot breath round right ear.

Spurt of irritation on my part. 'Why didn't you write? Or you could have rung me, you had the number.'

'It's better to come, isn't it? In person.'

It should have been. 'Stop it, Joel! I said, I don't want to.'

'You're out of practice, that's all. I'll soon get you back in the way of it.' Mumbling into my hair with his eyes shut, and busy fingers – wasn't there some horrible educational game for toddlers called that? Or a book of piano exercises played long ago by Tim? (He wasn't the pestering sort.) Joel's arms were pinioning mine. I trod hard on his foot.

'Leave me alone, will you?'

'No way – not after this distance!' And he tightened his grip, partly to tease, also to remind me that he was stronger.

We had progressed about the kitchen in this one-sided embrace, moving stiffly from step to step like partners on an overcrowded dance floor, until we were facing the glass-fronted cupboard where Rose kept her china. I noticed then that Joel was admiring not me, but his own reflection. But as I looked at him, I saw – different eyes, dark and wicked eyes, leering at me knowingly, out of his smiling face. So that I cried out and wrenching round, thumping him in the chest, brought up my knee. He let go and doubled up, coughing and swearing. I backed, eyeing him anxiously, wiping my mouth with my hand. I seemed to have hurt him a lot. He staggered to the sink and I was afraid he was going to be sick. After a minute he gulped some water straight from the tap.

'Sorry,' I said.

'What the hell's got into you,' he muttered.

'It's your fault. I told you to stop it.' I started to cry, hot miserable tears. I look hideous when I cry. I blubbered into a paper hanky, wiped off the surplus on my sleeve.

'Isn't that just typical!' he exclaimed thickly but triumphantly. 'She blames it all on me! I thought that was what you wanted. That's what you said in your letter. You ought to be more careful what you write, you could land yourself in trouble. Some blokes would take it out on you for what you did just then. Don't worry!' mockingly, as I flinched. 'I wouldn't touch you with gloves on, you aren't worth the trouble. You've lost weight,' he added, looking at me properly for the first time. I tried to speak, but he went on vindictively, 'It doesn't suit you. Nor does that colour. I've noticed before you look awful in brown.'

He wiped his face on Rose's towel and glared at me. This was the end, for us. I knew that he would never forgive me, but I felt curiously detached, as if it was all happening to other people. Perhaps they would hurt later, the remarks he now made to wound me as much as possible. He was as cruel as he could be in those dark minutes in the kitchen.

'Okay, I'm going,' he said at last, when he couldn't think of any more insults. He had covered most things, from my snobby family to my fluorescent socks. I hadn't spoken. I was noticing what a horrid shape his beautiful mouth made when he was being vile.

He took his scarf and I watched him out of the kitchen without a pang. He went through the baize door, crashing it shut behind him, rocking the old house whose vulnerable rooms were nervous of violence. Soon I heard him being angry in the passage, as if he couldn't find the way outside. By the time I got there he had opened a door, but it was the wrong one, and he had gone out not into the courtyard, but into that strip of garden I had looked down on so often from my bedroom. He was standing near the pond; he had his back to me but I could imagine his contemptuous, even outraged expression.

For the garden was derelict beyond belief. The ivy-covered wall bulged as if it would collapse at any moment, the yew hedge opposite it was more dead than alive. The pond was full of rubbish; if the moon had been reflected it was only by a broken pane of glass. There was no glass left in the windows of the summerhouse, and the door looked open because it had fallen in. Joel began walking that way, up the strip of untidy grass. I called after him, as loudly as I dared, 'Come back! You're trespassing,' and he must have heard, but he didn't stop.

The air was so cold that it hurt my nose and throat. I could only hope that Mrs Wadham was shut in with her dogs. For all I knew she was watching us from a window. I went after Joel, caught up with him as he reached the summerhouse. 'God, what a dump,' he said bitterly, without turning round. 'I don't know how you can stick it here, no wonder you've changed.'

He sounded muffled, somehow. That's to say, I could understand his words perfectly well, but my ears were tuned to noises beyond him, if there were any. I was looking beyond him, too, in case this ground-floor room wasn't empty, and it took my eyes a while to adjust to the long-undisturbed darkness. But soon I made out the stairs, just as I'd seen them in my dream, except that they were holey, and some of the banisters were missing.

Joel walked up the steps and began to climb the stairs. I said, 'Don't –' and then I gave up; I knew he'd go further if I tried to stop him. Besides, it was too late. The girl *was* here, in the shadow under the staircase. She seemed to be waiting, listening for someone; she was so preoccupied that she took no notice of us, but kept glancing anxiously at her watch. She was wearing the skirt and short-sleeved top I'd seen her in before. I wondered how she could bear it, in this weather. I was freezing myself without a coat.

I said, 'I'm sorry, my friend wanted to explore. We're trespassing I'm afraid.' She didn't answer. But now my eyes had adjusted to the darkness of the room and I could see her more clearly. To my horror, I realized that there were tears on her face, and suddenly she pressed the back of her hand to her mouth and actually sobbed. I couldn't bear it. I said, uselessly, 'I'm so sorry. Is there anything I can do?' But she didn't answer, or look at me or at Joel, who was coming downstairs.

He was staring at me. He said, 'Christy? Are you talking to me?' His voice still had that odd quality, as if he was speaking through a bath towel.

I didn't understand how he could be so thick. I made a face at him which was meant to convey, shut up for heaven's sake and let's get out of here. But it missed him completely. He took hold of my arm. 'Christy,' he said slowly, as if I was deaf or deranged, 'who are you talking to?'

'Come away!' I tried to leave the summerhouse, but he held me there.

'No way!' he said. 'I want to know who you think you're talking to. I want to know what the hell's going on round here.' Different programme – out of the soap opera into the police epic. I wanted to kick him. And all the time the girl went on being upset in her corner.

'If somebody's crying and you can't do anything about it, it's kinder to leave them alone,' I muttered.

'*Who's* crying? *What are you on about?*'

'My God, Joel, are you blind or what?'

'You're crazy!'

Then, even while I was looking at her, the girl – vanished.

86

I heard Joel from a great distance saying, 'You've gone as white as a sheet. What's the matter with you?'

I began trembling uncontrollably. My teeth were chattering. 'I'm cold, that's all.'

'You were talking to someone.'

'Forget it! I was fooling, I wanted to scare you.'

We walked side by side across the frosty grass. He said, 'You ought to get out of here before it's too late. When I get home I'll ring your parents, tell them to come and take you away.'

That made me furious. 'What's it got to do with you? Leave them out of it! They won't listen to you anyway.' But soon I calmed down, remembering they were still at Granny's, and that was a number he hadn't got.

Beyond the hedge there was an ancient tree dangling the remains of a swing. The bay window I had noticed from the field stuck out at an angle. The little stone sundial near it had a broken pointer, as if Mrs Wadham was no longer interested in the time of day.

As I was locking us into the passage, Rose's door bell rang so that I jumped and dropped the key. Joel let in dumbo Ed, all spots and witless grin.

'Sorry I'm late you guys, I lost the way. Again. Still you won't have missed me oi oi I think not. Hi, Christy!' (Leer, leer.)

'Hi.'

'Okay, let's go.' Joel pushed past me.

'Hey, hold it a minute, what about her? Aren't we taking her with us?'

Joel was walking out of my life. He'd nearly reached the gate. Ed turned to me, trying to understand what was going on. 'Hey, Christy, aren't we taking you to a party?'

'No.'

'But Joel said – Hey, has something happened between you two?'

'Get him to tell you about it.'

'Okay, thanks, Christy!' He was anxious to catch up with Joel, but he didn't want me to be sad. Several times he turned to wave and grin encouragingly at me as he made his hasty exit. I thought he would overbalance with kindness.

I went into the kitchen and lit the oven and crouched between it and the stove, trying to get warm. I wrote on a piece of paper: 'I don't understand what's happened to my great love' underlined three times exclamation marks. But I didn't get any further, now, or later in my diary. Personal passion stopped, for the time being, there.

The girl was a ghost. There was no way round that, no other name for a person who vanished under one's eyes. She wasn't help-spooks-panic, not at all; in fact her ghostliness explained certain anomalies, like her clothes and the music she played, which now fitted in with the date she had no doubt scratched on the window. But it did leave some basic questions unanswered, or even unanswerable.

If she was a ghost, so was Simon, and so was the third person in the triangle. Why had Rose never seen them? Why was I the victim? Possible answers brained out after two cups of coffee and intense if at times confused analytical thought: it might be something to do with the passion for Joel that I had brought into the house. Maybe that had made me receptive to them, and they had been able to use it as a way into my mind; they had fed on it in order to become visible to me for some reason. More and more often visible, and extinguishing by the way my own emotional relationship! But that was beside the point. The point now was, what could I do for them? I only knew, as I crouched there, hugging my knees and shivering between the two gas fires, that if I stayed I would find out. I knew that, with a supernatural certainty. If I stayed.

The telephone rang. It was Tim. He said they'd tried

several times and couldn't get through. Were we snowed up?

'No,' I said, surprised. 'It's clear as a bell here.' As I spoke I looked out of the window, and saw against the deepening early dusk of this December afternoon, one or two flakes drifting aimlessly down, as if they were trying out a different kind of weather.

'You're going to be,' he said cheerfully. 'We watched it on the telly chart. We've got a bit up here, but nothing like what's coming to you — masses of it.'

We had a friendly conversation about the Christmases we'd had, and thanked for our presents. Then Dad took over, and lastly Mum. She was already keen to get home.

'I don't think we'll be staying over New Year,' she told me. 'Granny's being impossible. Anyway we don't enjoy it much without you. How soon do you want to be fetched? I mean, we could come over today.'

'But it's much too late, you'd never get here before midnight!' I wasn't going to be hustled by one of Mum's rushes. And I didn't need the girl to remind me of my obligations – I had again that queer shiver, of the goose walking over my grave. 'Anyway, what about all this snow Tim's been telling me about? You might be stranded on the way.'

'You don't sound desperate to see us,' she said discontentedly. 'I gather you're having a good time.'

'Yes, it's okay. Have you got a pain?'

'My usual, Christmas pudding, I can never resist a second slice and then it does me in. You'd think the doctor could sort it out with his medical expertise but no.'

'Alka Seltzer.'

'That, dear, we forgot to bring, with the doctor's cufflinks and my little herb pillow. You know I can't sleep without it.'

'How was Tim's playing?'

'Very nice actually. Have you been doing any drawing?'

'A bit. I'm going to start something for Rose.'

She came in while we were still talking, with flakes of snow on her shoulders. (The weather was getting into its stride.) She was all of a glow so I knew where she'd been before she produced a treat for my supper, some slices of smoked salmon complete with sliver of lemon and a quarter of a bottle of rather nice white wine, set aside from Boxing Day luncheon. I was very glad to have it. When I thought about it, it was the only food I'd taken in all day.

Rose sat and talked while I started on the tiny portrait. That snap had been taken when they went to Italy in the summer – had she mentioned that they'd been on holiday together? Nothing *like that*, of course, they'd just travelled together, as friends, and done the same things because that was what they enjoyed doing. Well they'd actually ended up staying in the same hotel, because Huntley hadn't been happy in the one the travel agent booked for him, but they'd had separate rooms of course because she was old-fashioned and luckily so was Huntley. Sometimes circumstances made one behave in a way that was unconventional but after all it didn't matter what other people thought, as long as one didn't do anything wrong.

I listened, and drew and rubbed out and drew his tiny outline. It would have to be marriage for Rose and Huntley, and looking at her tonight I began to feel hopeful; but perhaps it was only the euphoria of Christmas. What they needed was a drama – something to jolt them out of the old rut, into each other's arms.

Later, she invited me to spend tomorrow with her in the shop. She had to go in although they weren't open, to mark things down for the sale and rearrange the shelves. We could have a picnic lunch, and then Huntley had asked us both over in the evening, to eat up the last of the turkey.

I made agreeable remarks. But I had a premonition that I wouldn't be available tomorrow. Surely if the snow came, it would change everything –

I had a dream that was a dream. It was night, and there was one of those huge wheels you have at fairs with seats all round the rim. All the places were taken by people I knew – my family, Rose and Huntley, Joel, my friends – they were all there. Then the gaudy lights went on, and the harsh blare of the fair music started to play, and the wheel began to turn. Little by little it gathered speed, until it was whizzing round like a firework. And then, if the people clinging to it let go, they were flung off to travel strangely slowly among the stars which were shining very bright and low in the sky. But not many took the risk. They mostly clung, laughing or shrieking, to the fairground wheel.

I knew that beyond all I could see in the dream, there loomed something of infinitely greater importance, something indefinable but constant, as it might be an immense Pattern or Design. Within it, this fairground drama had a fractional but indispensable place. The people on the wheel were not puppets. Each had his or her supernatural significance, and eternal position within the Whole. But for each it was necessary to make the journey away from the wheel.

Then I longed for just a glimpse of all that which was out of sight. I knew that if only I could hold on to my dream for long enough, the chance would come, there would be a chink. I understood (in this dream) that just a glimpse of the Whole would touch everything, even after I woke, with its purpose and beauty. But alas, there was no way of stopping the wheel, and I was on it too, and its whirling was making me sick. So I woke up too soon, wrung with disappointment.

I got out of bed and went to the window to cool my head against the glass. It was the middle of the night. The garden between the wall and the hedge lay pure, unbroken white. Isolated upon it, at a distance from each other, three dark figures made a triangular pattern. They were turned towards the squat tower of the summerhouse against the snow-filled wood. No moonshine tonight; the frozen pond had the dull glare of a blind eye. The three stood on that oblong of snow as if they had dropped out of the stars, without footprints or shadows. The snow was like a blank page waiting to be written – they would choose, and make their indelible marks, make them for ever. For who can fix the ending to anything that happens?

Next morning I joined Rose for breakfast in my nightclothes, with the idea of going back to bed for more sleep; but first I waved her off from the back door. And there was the courtyard, transformed out of this world – fitted with a white velvety blanket, all patterned with tiny bird footmarks, and the yews drooping over it, heavily crusted with snow. Rose crept away in her white-mufflered car, daring the elements – or anything – for her date with Huntley. Her last words to me were, 'No, it'll turn to rain by lunchtime, we never get much snow in these parts,' but I looked up at the packed sky and I didn't believe her. I ran upstairs and dressed, and rushed out again. I rolled snowballs and hurled them up into the trees. I made a snowman with a big nose and a twig fringe – he looked like Huntley. I shouted and danced, there was no one to see. For the snow made everything so beautiful. The ugly outside plumbing had been transformed to white geometry down the front of the house. The roofs looked like cloaks and wimples. The chimney stacks looked like bride cake.

By the time I went indoors to get warm, it had started

snowing again. I tried Granny's number, but the line was dead. Somewhere between here and Hemel Hempstead, communications had broken under the weight of snow. If Mum had her way, they might turn up on the doorstep any moment to take me home, but I didn't expect them. I guessed they were huddled indoors with the snowfall rising outside the windows. Dad would hardly notice it; Mum always gave him thrillers for Christmas and he would read his way through. Tim would play computer games. But Mum would be bored, bored, biting her nails, making a mess of the crossword, going into a different room to stare out of a different window. Eventually Dad would finish reading and raise his head and say, 'I've got to go into the hospital tomorrow,' and the weather would clear miraculously so that he could. (I used to believe that this happened; when I was small I believed that he was in control of things which ruled the lives of the rest of us.) Or he might say, 'I'm going to pick up Christy tomorrow.' But Mum had given him several books, and he wasn't a quick reader.

I had a packet soup for lunch and a lot of hot buttered toast. Then I went out again in a lull between snowfalls. Huntley had grown. I gave him a stick with which to measure the aesthetic centre point of oyster-coloured space in order to hang Rose's Christmas present; I had forgotten his eyebrows, and added more twigs. Then I went on to the farm. The darkness of the laurels was white, white, all their boughs were weighted, bending earthwards, dunking me with snow as I pushed between them, wading on with my snow-stuffed boots, snow-caped, snow-capped. I'd never been out in country snow and I was unprepared for this immense whiteness, scarcely interrupted by the horizon because the sky was so nearly the colour of the land; the almost complete obliteration of detail, bar mapping-pen-patterned trees and hedges and above all the silence, or a

94

single bird voice clear across a width of muffled fields.

The calves were excited by the change in the weather, and crammed up to the railings in their dark and steamy shed. I was horrified to see Peter lying prone in the yard. I thought he'd fallen and hurried towards him, but then I saw that he'd levered up the stone slab with the ring in it, and he was lowering a bucket into what I had rightly guessed was the well. I could hear him muttering and swearing as I approached. I squatted opposite and stared down. The well was more of a crypt, stone-lined; deeper, wider than anyone could see. The bucket dangled on a rope.

He raised his scarlet face and looked at me sternly. 'Keep back! If you fall in here you won't come out alive mind!'

And he had another go at throwing down the bucket with sufficient force to break the surface of the water, but it wasn't heavy enough. He was losing his temper, and much likelier to fall in than I was. I remembered the pitchfork in the shed, for spreading straw in the pen. I fetched it and a sack I found there, spread the sack, lay on it on my face, found the inside of the wobbly bucket with the end of the pitchfork handle, and pushed. I could feel the resistance of that black and icy water, but suddenly it gave and the bucket sank with a rush, as if it was being grabbed from below. We filled the trough for the calves and snugged it round with straw to keep it from freezing. Peter bedded the pen with extra straw, and stuffed more in the racks.

'Got any water over at the house?' he asked me.

'Just the one tap.'

'That'll be in the kitchen. I've never known that tap to freeze, not in all my years at Wadham's.'

'What about Mrs Wadham? Is she okay?'

'Was this morning, when I took in her milk.'

'Rose is going to get the plumber out.'

He stared at me, as if I was an idiot.

'*Get the plumber out!*' he repeated scornfully. 'There won't be no coming and going round here, not for a day or two. We'll be cut right off by nightfall if not sooner. Shouldn't think – ' he pushed back his cap, spoke with a grim satisfaction – 'shouldn't think there'll be any coming and going whatever, not before next week. At the earliest.'

'But they'll clear the roads and put down grit, won't they?'

'Not Christmas week they won't. *Put down grit*!' he again repeated with a cheerless laugh. 'I should like to see them. With a yard of cattle to feed when the tractor won't start, and the water frozen in the pipes. 'Tis bad every year, and most years worse than others.'

But if the plumber couldn't get through, what about Rose? How could she come home, assuming that she had reached town safely this morning? We were cut off. *I* was cut off – if not now, by nightfall.

Peter didn't actually thank me for my help, but before he went away he did tell me that I could always come up his place if I needed anything. And in the circumstances, that was nice to know.

The dead white sky was opening again, the flakes falling. Each had its noiseless, weightless place in my imprisonment. They felt like blind fingertips trying to identify my face. I went back to the house, I'd left the door wide open so perhaps it was full of burglars as well as ghosts. A large black bird had got into the passage, a rook I supposed; it had panicked and knocked down some jars. I shepherded it through the doorway and it flew low across the snow, veered sharply up into a tree. The lowering sky seemed almost balancing on Huntley's by now disproportionately long head. He was buried to the armpits and his measuring stick had fallen from his hand. I went in, locking the door. The passage was almost dark. All I could do was wait for Rose's frantic phone call – if she managed to get through.

Ring, ring. 'Hallo?'

'Is that you, Christy?' Who else? Did the girl ghost answer the phone?

'Yes, it is, and that's you, Rose.'

'Listen, I'm at Huntley's, I don't know what to do, I can't get home.' Maiden-auntly anxiety well conveyed.

'No, you can't possibly. It's been snowing here most of today.'

'But are you *all right*?'

'Yes, of course. I'm fine. Don't worry.'

'Oh dear, oh dear, I don't like the thought of you being marooned out there all alone!'

'I'm not alone.' Not at all. 'There's Mrs Wadham next door, and I can walk up to Peter's, he said to do that if I needed anything.'

'Oh dear, what would Susan say?'

'She wouldn't say anything. Why should she? It's not your fault.'

'Well, no, but I feel responsible.'

And I thought, she'll go on fussing about these details, because she's afraid to grasp what's important. Although she wants it so desperately, she's afraid. I could see very clearly the star-spangled opportunity for her and Huntley, and how the wheel would turn, and how the chance could be lost.

'Are you there?' she said.

It suddenly struck me that she needed me, and I spoke as I wouldn't have done without my dream, and the empty house round me, the snow and ghosts – this bizarre background forced out truths. 'Listen, Rose. It's a *good thing*, you and Huntley. I'm sure,' I said.

'I'm not making excuses to stay here, if that's what you think.'

Oh exasperating aunt. 'I know that. But here is the snow and you must take advantage of it.'

Poignant silence.

'Rose? You and Huntley. *Don't waste it.*'

We waited. Then at the same time we put down our receivers: not angrily, but because there was nothing more to say. I went into the kitchen and made some coffee, and sat down to finish Huntley's picture while I waited for what would happen next.

I slept at the kitchen table with my head on my arms and my hair in the paintbox. There were too many dimensions to that house and I didn't want to risk going upstairs, not in my solitary state. So that was where I was when I was woken by several tremendous thumps on the dividing door.

I jerked upright. Huntley's likeness, propped against the dirty coffee mug, surveyed the kitchen, sunburnt and relaxed. I thought there had been thumps. The silence seemed still echoing with them. I went out into the hall. Whoever had thumped had been listening for that. Impatient fingers rattled the handle.

I said, tentatively, 'Mrs Wadham?'

'Open the door, open the door!' she said.

I hesitated. Then I did.

She was standing right up to the door, in the dark, the nearest light just a glow behind her from the second room where the piano was. And she seemed to fill the doorway: tall, thin, wrecked as the skeleton of a ship caught offshore, tide after tide. She glared at me, propped on her rubber-ended stick, thrusting forward a kettle with one hand.

'Do you want some water?'

She didn't answer. I took the kettle, carried it into the kitchen and filled it from our single functional tap. All the way there and back, along passages, through walls, I was conscious of her following, devouring eyes.

'Okay? Is there anything else you need?'

'You can give me some milk.'

A voice that grated, like a rusty key turning in a dry lock.

99

There was some milk in the fridge. I went to fetch it. She couldn't manage her stick and the kettle and the milk. As I stepped forward to accompany her to wherever she was living in that bleak house, she made a jab with her crutch at the fateful dividing door, so that it slammed shut behind us. And that, for me, was the blindfold leap into God knew what was coming.

Dust, mould in the plummy drawing-room, no smell of roses here. It had the cold dampness of a grave. On the mantelpiece, the cobwebbed floral tribute suitably crowned the death mask in white marble.

She jabbed again as we passed the second door. Its slam cut off, for the second time, any retreat, and echoing over us, vanished in the shadows beyond the piano – the broken-down instrument Rose had been so angry about. Our pace was deadly slow. With every step the water slopped from the kettle, as Mrs Wadham swivelled and thumped.

The walls were gloomy with pictures of dead views, the room with heavy rectangular pieces of furniture, the shapes and weight of tombs, which marked out a sort of obstacle course for Mrs Wadham. For a while we got on more quickly, as she passed herself with practised speed from the corner of a chest to the back of an armchair and so to the sideboard, from there to the table, and on to the back of another chair, with her crutch clopping the furniture and much loss from the spout. Her progress was assessed by the bland face of a stopped grandfather clock, tilted forward in a suggestive manner like an upended coffin. We turned down a long stone-flagged passage, unlit but for the rectangular outline of a door at the end, indicating that the lamp was on in that room. There her dogs waited and whined, and when I opened the door they rushed out. The door was on a spring so that it would close automatically. I held it while the three got themselves back inside, then I let it go. Mrs Wadham and the dogs and I were shut in together. I said, 'Where shall I put the milk?'

It was a good question. Mrs Wadham was now living entirely in this one room, judging by the cooking arrangements (two electric rings and a toaster) and the crimson-counterpaned and cushioned divan. Her pictures were mostly Impressionist; her books, covering one wall, mostly paperbacks. Had it not been solid Victorian, the mantelpiece might have given way under the weight of a Christmas cactus sprouting pink feathery flowers, a teapot, milk jug and bag of sugar, a mug with GO printed red on black, a small Chinese cabinet with doors and drawers, a black and gold clock (stopped), a china model of girl with dog ('thirties at a guess), peacock feathers in a filigree metal container, a box of dog chocks, and a jar of Olde Englishe marmalade; plus a few Christmas cards, one upside down, a stack of unopened letters, and a tin tray, modern, with a shiny reproduction of Queen Victoria on it.

Mrs Wadham was across the room by this time, and working her way towards the bay window where an old-fashioned, comfortable armchair was standing beside a table with books and a telephone on it. The curtains were tomato-coloured and hung in strips not quite wide enough for the windows, so that slices of midnight garden still showed, with a white fur trimming of snow. There was a standard lamp in the window, and another near the fireplace, heavily shaded and trimmed; the ceiling light had a pink glass bowl, spotted with dead flies. The dogs climbed politely on to a sofa covered with faded and stained brocade, whose canine smell reached me where I was standing at the door. Mrs Wadham too sat down. 'Shall we have tea?' she suggested, as though she had only to press a bell, and a maid in theatrical cap and apron would come in with a tray.

I found the flex and put on the kettle. Tea and chocolate biscuits I discovered among the articles on the mantelpiece, and there were clean cups and saucers 'n a cupboard, bone china they were, with a flower pattern. All this I arranged on the tray, and carried it to the table. 'Do you take sugar?'

'Two, or perhaps three.'

She watched me stir them in, and taking the cup with both hands, blew greedily until it was cool enough to suck between her purplish lips. All the time she kept her eyes on me. And they were still striking, in her wrecked face – large, deep-set, very blue.

'Aren't you going to sit down?' she snapped unexpectedly.

'Okay.' I looked round. It seemed simplest to sit on the floor. 'Okay, okay!' she repeated, mockingly. I finished my biscuit and took another. When she had drunk her tea I took her cup and she looked at me within reach and remarked, 'There is a great distance between us.'

'Yes.' I thought I knew what she meant.

'Put down the cup. No, I don't want any more.' She began fumbling among the books on the table by her elbow; I grabbed the telephone before it crashed to the ground. She pulled out an envelope, passed it to me, stared me in the face while I looked at it, as if she was trying to catch me out. She said, 'You've seen that man?'

'Yes,' I said. It was the drawing I'd done for Peter. She hadn't looked at the card inside, the envelope was still sealed. She changed her position in the chair with a jerk and a grimace. There was a suppressed violence about her now, that the pain of walking had dissipated. There was more wolf than Red Riding Hood granny in her face.

'You've seen him here?' she demanded, sharply. 'Is that what you mean?'

'Yes.'

'Ah.' And she sighed, as though this confirmed the existence of a suspected obstacle that would have to be negotiated. 'I thought so. That was what I wanted to know.'

We sat in silence for several minutes. The electric radiators, on which various stockings and unidentifiable grubby underclothes were airing, made no noise. The dogs were quiet.

She said, 'I thought he would come back – if he ever went away in the first place.' I could add nothing to this. She suddenly exclaimed, very loudly and bitterly, 'It isn't easy to shuffle off what's past!'

I wondered what I would do if she had a stroke or a heart attack. I couldn't get the doctor out. I would have to follow telephoned instructions. It would be like the two men who lived on a lighthouse. When one died, by the time the other was relieved, at the end of a wild winter, he was a raving lunatic. I wondered if it was a medical fact that one's hair could turn white in a night. The warm atmosphere and bright lights were making me sleepy and confused. Now and then I looked surreptitiously at Mrs Wadham. She sat with her head back, her eyes closed, apparently asleep except for her fingers which plucked and plucked at the fringed arms of the chair. I jumped when she asked abruptly, without opening her eyes, 'What time is it?'

I tried to make sense of my watch. 'Twenty to two.'

'Take the divan, take it, I shall sleep here.'

I was glad to be allowed out of range of her salvo-style conversation. There were various garments I had to remove from the divan before I could lie down on it: robes of kimono and dressing-gown type in brilliant colours, kingfisher blue, emerald green, tangerine and poppy. After some thought, not liking to ask, I draped them carefully over the unoccupied end of the dogs' sofa. I didn't want to get between her sheets. I didn't know how clean they would be; there is dirt and dirt. I lay on top of the covers, and to keep me warm I took a heavy dark-brown coat of glistening fur out of a cupboard. Meanwhile Mrs Wadham never stirred, except for her fingers. I could see the top of her untidy grizzled head over the back of the chair. As soon as I shut my eyes I floated away, to circle the ceiling like a summer moth round the ugly pink shade. I lay like that through what was left of the night. You could hardly call it sleep, a sound from Mrs Wadham or the dogs would have roused me immediately; but it was surprisingly refreshing.

The room looked dingy when I came to, and the lamps wan. Mrs Wadham's eyes were open but abstracted; she was far in thought from this room. Her lips moved now and then in a definite way, as if she was reaching conclusions. Behind her, on the sofa, Madman and Spectre blinked and stretched themselves. I drew back the curtains and noticed within the bay window a narrow glass door that would open into the garden. I let out the dogs and clapped it shut quickly, for the cold cut in like a knife. After they were in again, I took the empty kettle and dirty teapot through to Rose's part to wash and fill. I was upstairs in the bathroom when I heard the gate, and looking out, saw Peter struggling with it against the snow. He was carrying a can. I ran downstairs and opened the door before he reached it; I hate being jangled by a bell when I'm alone in a house, even at home.

He pushed back his cap and stared at the snowman and grinned, and then he offered me the can. 'Do you need any milk?'

'Thanks – I'll take it through to Mrs Wadham.'

'If you do that, it'll save me a trip. I've had your auntie on the phone.'

'Was she in a fuss?'

'You could call it that. I've got her number, said I'd ring back.' He looked at me shrewdly. 'I thought the old girl would have you out.'

'That's why Rose couldn't get me.'

'That's what I thought. There's a pie in her cupboard, bread and butter and that, Lily sees to all that for her. So help yourself. She don't eat much. She'll always drink a cup of tea.'

'Okay. She's a bit absent-minded this morning.'

'Been like it years. If you'm worried, you've only got to press the button on top of the phone by her chair, that'll put you through to us direct. One or other of us'll be in all day.'

'Okay. Do you want any help with the water on the farm?'

'Not today – I done all that while you was still asleep!'

He took something dark and heavy out of his pocket and passed it across to me. It had a cold feel. I saw that it was a heavy clasp knife with the blade open, rusted round the hinge.

'What's it made of? Not wood, is it?'

'No – wood would've rotted all away. That's horn. That were a handsome knife when I saw it last. That come up in the bucket this morning.'

'Out of the well, you mean? Is it yours?'

'No. Nor it didn't belong to the Captain. I know who it did belong to though. Makes you wonder what else is lying down there.'

It was very cold in the courtyard. The coldness was creeping up me, chilling my veins. I gave back the knife. He turned it in his hands, remembering.

''Twere that dry that summer, the horses had to be watered out of the tank. Lucas did that, he had a way with horses, nor he never wanted no help. He even slept with the things. Made his bed in the hay, he did, never wanted no sheets like a Christian man.'

Cold, far colder than if I was made of snow, I stood there listening to him.

'He stopped with us a year, and that were a year too long for most of us. He left the same day as the Captain. Maybe he joined the army, maybe he didn't. We never heard. Nobody didn't hear nothing of him, not from that day to this.'

He dropped the knife into his pocket, and turned to go. 'Captain Wadham, he was a good man,' he said. 'I'd like to think he put things right, before he went away.'

He trudged off. I went in with the milk.

Mrs Wadham was still sitting in her armchair, as if she hadn't moved all the time I was away. Even her fingers were motionless, and the horrible thought occurred to me that she might be dead. My heart began to beat fast and I had to force myself to walk round the chair into the bay of the window, but the stole slightly moving across her breast indicated that she was still breathing. The colour of it – Christmas scarlet – somehow emphasized her ravaged old age. It was my first chance to have a proper look at her.

Granny had a marshmallow prettiness – there was nothing of that in this old face. Only her eyes, deep-set under her fierce brow, suggested beauty; otherwise every line, every feature seemed in conflict, even when she was asleep. The battles in her life had been too harsh, she had lost too much. But her expression wasn't defeated. She had never given up, and there was still a desperate hopefulness in her face. It was hard going, though. Her unconscious fingers were crooked as if she was grasping the arms of the chair.

The only jewellery she wore was a wide gold wedding ring, fixed for ever under the swollen joint of her fourth finger, and a gold watch on a linked gold bracelet on her left wrist. I had seen that watch before. Suddenly, I caught my breath, raised my eyes to her face.

When she was young, Cynthia Wadham had run up the summer-house stairs, on fire with love. And at that moment she opened her eyes, as if I had called her out of sleep. I saw at once that I should have recognized the blue.

She began talking at once, as if we were in the middle of a conversation. 'It's very odd, but I have the feeling we knew each other, a long time ago. Isn't that strange?' She looked at me pleasantly. 'Do you remember Simon, my husband?'

'I've seen him several times.'

'He was killed during the war. That was the greatest grief of my life.'

There was silence. There wasn't anything comforting to say: it would have been like giving weak tea to a tiger.

'I was a very pretty girl,' she remarked in a different tone. Then she laughed scornfully. 'I haven't looked in a mirror for years, I've no idea what I look like now and none of that matters, but when I started out I was beautiful. It was hard for me to settle here in the back of beyond. No, I'm not making excuses, but I was very lonely, and then I had ideas about love. Girls did then – perhaps it's different today.'

'It's the same,' I said.

'I'm afraid I wasn't patient. Simon would behave like a gentleman. He was afraid of upsetting me. Ridiculous! –Are you shocked?'

'Not in the least.'

'Of course not, anyway we've talked about this before. You see he never allowed himself to be carried away, and that's humiliating. That's the last thing he meant, but it was. Do you understand?'

'Yes, I think so.'

'He never talked about love. It was something that happened in the dark. Sometimes he even apologised. And no babies –'

She braced her spine against the back of the chair, closed her eyes. She said after a minute, 'Simon must have known what was going on with Lucas, he should have tried to stop

108

it. For my sake. That was the crowning humiliation.'

Madman or Spectre yawned and changed position on the sofa. Then the room was silent for a while. She suddenly said, in a cracked, pitiful voice, 'I never had the chance to tell him I was sorry, that all that was a mistake. . . .' The crack between her eyelids leaked a tear down her thin cheek.

I made some tea. Lily's pie was good, but Mrs Wadham wouldn't touch it. She didn't talk any more. The morning had been misty, but later the weather cleared, and the snow looked so pretty that I decided to go for a walk. The whippets wanted to come, but I was afraid she would miss them, and they were useful as guards.

I walked briskly down the field. The frosted snow crunched underfoot, formed fairy-tale billows where it had drifted under the trees. The stream had frozen in the act of flowing from rock to rock; its suspended fall looked like the glass pipes of some magical instrument. But the voice of the water had been cut off, and the voices of birds. The only sound was my footsteps. Nothing else moved in that still, snow-bound country.

I followed the path to the wood. Quite a lot of snow had been fielded by the thin arms of the trees, making white nests which occasionally fell with a soft crash. I looked up. The sky was still hazy round the topmost branches. And those branches were – surely? – green! And while I stared up at them, I sensed that the snow scene was shrinking, drawing away behind me. Fade up birdsong, bumble bee buzz, delicate scent of wild flowers – it had happened again: I had moved abruptly without any doorway, without the least warning, into that other world. The wood was all leafy and green. The air that had held a frozen silence was now alive under the trees.

I stood looking round for several minutes, and then I walked on along the path. Soon I came out on the far side of the wood above the old railway cutting. But now there was a track, a shining double line curving out of sight, with a signal gantry partly visible beyond the trees. It was a very hot afternoon though the sky was cloudy. The rails shimmered. Then I heard a distinct clunk! as the signal in the distance changed from green to red, and my heartbeat slipped into a higher gear, as feelings of anticipation mounted in my chest. The rails began to hum, to vibrate. The vibration increased until it sounded as though they were trying to wrench away from the sleepers, and then with a sudden roar, the dolly train appeared clicketty-click round the curve of the wood. The engine was green with bright brass trim, and puffed grey smoke. The driver braked; the train squealed, slowed, squealed to a stop.

I was standing opposite the last of the chocolate-and-yellow compartments. There was only one person inside – a young man with a kit bag on the seat beside him. When the train stopped, he got up and came to the window. It was Simon. He looked back along the line, and then he looked into the wood. Then he returned to his place. Still the light showed red, though the train panted with impatience. Simon's head was bent, he seemed deep in thought. He shifted his position, looked drearily across at the brown photographs of holiday resorts on the opposite wall under the luggage rack. I watched him with desperate attention. I was suddenly aware of words going through my mind – you can't let her go, you can't let her go, I was thinking in railway rhythm.

Just as the signal changed from red to green, he came to a decision. He caught up his bag, thrust open the door and jumped lightly down on to the embankment. It was done in a moment, and the door slammed after him; nobody saw him, I could have told him that. He climbed up the slope without hesitation, as if he'd already worked out this alternative plan, shoved his bag into a bramble patch and set off down the footpath to Wadham's.

I had difficulty keeping up with him, for he ran until he could see the house. Then he was careful to hide, picking his way rapidly under the trees which grew more thickly now along the banks of the stream, and making a wide detour in the cover of a sprawling hedge until he was safely into the wood at the top of the garden. My heart was beating horribly, not only because I was out of breath. I guessed where he was going and I knew that I must try to warn Cynthia; I was afraid for her, very afraid. I was too tired to run any more, so trusting in my invisibility I took the shortest way straight through the gardens.

The house was like Peter's picture come to life, except that a black-and-white version could give no idea of the smouldering glory of the scarlet creeper covering the walls. There was a tennis court, and deck chairs out, but no one to be seen. Yet the swing hanging from a tree was still moving, as though someone had just got up from it, because there was no wind at all that sultry afternoon.

The air was so oppressive, I could hardly get my breath. My heart was pounding like a sledge hammer. As I reached the pond, its surface was suddenly broken by a plop, and raising my face, I felt another, heavy drop of warm rain. This was the garden of dreams, a scented place with all the roses in full bloom along the wall, and the lawn mown to a billiard-table smoothness. Swallows zipped to and fro. The sky hung full to bursting overhead, and the lawn seemed impossibly long as I struggled with nightmare slowness over it. I thought I caught a glimpse of Simon in the wood.

He emerged from the trees just ahead of me, and soundlessly climbing the two steps to the summerhouse, paused with his hand on the door. It was closed, but not fastened. He pushed it ajar, and slipped inside. I hesitated. At that moment there was a rumble of thunder directly over the wood. The storm was about to break, and I crept in after him. He was standing at the bottom of the stairs, looking up. His face looked pale in the half-light.

Somebody moved on the first floor. Then Cynthia spoke with terrible distinctness. She said, 'No – please stop it! You mustn't do that!' On paper the words might be a refusal. They didn't sound like one. She was nervous, but she was very excited – she hadn't been taken upstairs by force. Listening to her, I felt myself starting to blush. Simon's hand clenched over the banister. I couldn't bear to look at his face. There was a bit of a silence. Then she laughed, a little embarrassed, very keyed up. 'No – no, I can't!' Light movements of feet overhead, very close to each other, and to us for that matter. 'Don't do that – I can't let you behave like this!' almost whispering – followed by pressure on the creaky floor, and a gasping cry, part fear, part love, cut short, by his lips probably.

Suddenly there was an almighty crack of thunder, that seemed to explode inside the summerhouse, holding it for an instant in a glare of light. Then all went black, as the crammed clouds opened in torrents of rain. Simon paused for a moment in the doorway. Then he went out into the garden, and I followed; we were drenched between one end of the lawn and the other. As we approached the house a woman darted from the bay window, pulled in the deckchairs, slammed the door shut. It was providential that she didn't see Simon who was moving as if in a daze, as if he was sleepwalking. As he rounded the corner of the house, a sopping, sobbing, shivering creature hurled itself at him – it was his whippet, Phantom. He stooped to pet her and talk to her, before he thrust her inside through the door where, years later, I was to push that fateful Christmas card. I heard her whining piteously as I passed.

We went into the farm by a different gate. The yard was clean, the buildings trim; in the one I knew as a calfhouse, there was a pony trap covered with a cloth with its shafts stuck up in the air. I sheltered in there, while Simon stood in the stable doorway, smoking one cigarette after another. It was still pouring with rain. The sky was only a shade lighter than the slate roofs of the buildings. I knew he was waiting for Lucas. Fear lay like a dead hand on my shoulder.

At last we heard whistling, and Lucas came through the red door in the archway. He was smiling, soaked through, his shirt clinging to his muscular shoulders and arms. He saw Simon at once, and hesitated just for a step; then he walked on with deliberate, insolent ease. His gypsy hair, shiny with wet, curled to the nape of his strong brown neck. He slid his right hand, the one nearest me, into his trousers pocket.

Simon chucked away his cigarette and crossed the yard to meet him. He spoke, but I couldn't hear what he said. He punched Lucas in the face.

It was horrible to see how they hated each other. They were fighting to kill, beating at each other with sickening thumps, gasping for breath, cursing as they struggled to keep their footing on the slippery cobbles. Simon was quicker, but not as strong. He had to keep out of Lucas's clutch; he could do it, but only while he was fresh. They circled like wrestlers, breathing hard. It was then I caught the glint of the knife in Lucas's hand. He was grinning through blood bursting from his nose. 'Old school tie!' he croaked, jeering, and he lunged and grabbed Simon by the collar. The muscles bulged in his arm as he tightened his stranglehold. Simon was choking, uselessly struggling. Lucas bent over him, dark, bloody, gloating; he raised the steel blade to Simon's neck –

In their rage, both men had forgotten that the cover was off the well. Lucas stepped back – and dropped, with a hideous cry. Simon was hurled across the cobbles.

The scene began to shrink, slip back through time. I

heard the horses panicky in the stable, when Simon staggered in for a rope. I heard the secret drains, that were already feeding the cavern with rainwater, making a hollow chuckling noise, as if someone deep inside was enjoying a joke. I heard the cover come down like the lid of a tomb.

Around me the wintry trees were closing in, in their landscape of snow. The air was suddenly so cold, it was difficult to breathe. The line of my footsteps stopped where I was standing. I followed them back to the house.

Peter came round to feed the dogs, and gave me a message from Rose: her love and to say that she would be over in the morning. (That was when she told me how Huntley had remembered he had a pair of skis in the loft. She had been practising all day, up and down his garden while he stood on the steps drinking wine and calling out encouragement and instructions.) I was glad that Peter saw Mrs Wadham. To me, she looked different, even more distracted, as if her mind was now mostly fixed on something a long way away. She was like a traveller whose thoughts are all on the country waiting at the end of the voyage. But he was reassuring. She often looked like that, he said.

He would talk about her to me, as if she was too far gone to understand him. She did though, I could tell from the sharp way she glanced at him now and then. But she had more important things on her mind.

After he had left, she suddenly asked me to put on the gramophone. It was a very old portable, with a handle to wind before it would start, and a heavy pick-up with a metal needle. I found a stack of records, seventy-eights, old dance tunes and pop songs of the 'thirties. The wonder was that the gramophone still worked. We drank tea to the Cole Porter medley I'd heard her playing on the piano in the beginning. Sometimes her knotty old fingers tapped out the tunes, while the cold sky darkened, drawing the colour from the frozen garden, blotting out the shapes she had sat looking at, year after year.

'That's enough!' she said curtly, when she was tired of it.

115

'That's enough, that's enough!' I lifted the needle from the record before it was finished, and put everything away.

Time passed – half an hour or more, before she spoke again.

'Are you going to stay?'

I looked up from the novel I'd taken from the shelf. 'Yes.'

'Good.'

By and by she asked, 'Are you still there?'

'Yes.'

'I wish you'd come and sit over here where I can see you,' she said fretfully.

I got off the divan and sat on the floor in the bay of the window. 'Do you want the curtains drawn?'

'No, no, leave them open. I'm looking out tonight.'

It was black dark. But her face was busy, as though scenes were being re-enacted for her, on the dark screens of the windowpanes.

After another long while, she became abstracted again. I looked at her between chapters, and wondered what it was that filled her mind. 'Would you like something to drink?'

She mumbled, 'Don't interrupt.'

I got up to stretch my legs and find something to eat. The room was warm, in spite of the weather; that was what Rose needed, electric radiators. I took some milk and a packet of biscuits to my place, and went on reading. All the same, I kept an eye on Mrs Wadham. However still she was, however absorbed, she wasn't relaxed.

I looked up, feeling her attention had returned to me. She was completely herself again and gave me a smile. 'Will you be able to stay awake all night?' she asked courteously, as if she was inviting me to walk round the garden, or have another cup of tea. 'I know it's a great deal to ask, when you're so young. But it's so good of you to keep watch for me – while I'm away, so to speak.'

'Yes, I will.' I did feel curiously alert, far from comfortable on the floor, but not minding that – minding much more about being a part of whatever was going on.

That pleased her. She asked for lemon squash, and swallowed a mouthful – it was the last refreshment she took before the journey. After that I looked up several times to meet her gaze, when she was smiling at me almost tenderly. At last she seemed to sleep. But I didn't sneak off to the divan, I kept my word, only sometimes walked about, to relieve the cramps in my legs.

When she woke up she exclaimed, 'How beautiful you are! How odd that it never struck me before! You're a beautiful, beautiful girl!' The words weren't quite clear, they were fuzzy with whatever bright dream she had had. Hearing her tone of wonder and excitement, the two dogs left their bed and walked up to her chair, on the right and the left of her. She put down both hands to fondle them. She smiled down. 'My beautiful, beautiful dogs!' It was as if everything she saw was suddenly shot through with glory – a virtue not in us, but coming from herself. The dogs seemed to sense it, and want to prolong it. They settled down beside her, couched in the position hounds have on tombs. Now and then I surprised a pale eye staring across at me.

So we passed into the next phase of that night. We were tightly grouped, we four living things. And that was good, because soon after midnight the wind must have got up; at any rate something was bumping against the outside of the house, like a big night bird that had lost its sense of direction. The noise seemed to trouble Mrs Wadham. She moved her head restlessly to and fro on the high back of the chair, and muttered, 'I don't want that other to come.' She clasped her poor old hands and repeated, more urgently and clearly, 'I don't want him to come!'

'He won't,' I said.

'How can you tell? No one can be sure of that!'

I thought the room was colder, and I found a shawl and covered her legs. For myself I put on the fur coat – what beast had worn it once? It didn't match anything I had ever seen in a zoo. Her head was still moving restlessly on the chair. I touched her hand. She grasped mine, and held on to it. 'Will Simon meet me?' she asked like a child.

'Yes.'

There was a long silence, softly interrupted now and then by the buffeting of wings or wind.

'Surely he knows how sorry I've been, all these years!' she suddenly cried out.

Then I had the distinct impression that her little boat was leaving the shore. For soon she went back to sleep, but this time allowed her head to droop into the angle the wing made with the chair. Her hands became limp and clammy, and when I felt her pulse it was as small as the flutter of a dying bird.

I must have slept with my head on the arm of her chair. When I woke, the window was lightening, and the silhouette of wood and hill stood clearly against the sky. The air was as still as if the whole world, in the unblemished whiteness of the snow, awaited the coming of day. It was a thin time and a very cold time, when the darkness was running out before the chariot of the sun. The night was being shattered by luminous vibrations.

And now the sky was warming to pink, which was softly reflected by the snow. The rimed trees began to glitter; the ropes of the old swing were furry with frost. The end of the field was cut off by a bar of mist, on which the tops of the tallest trees floated like islands.

I turned back to the garden, and there was Simon. He was standing on the lawn, watching us. He was radiant, as if his veins were full of light instead of blood. He had come, but as I looked round at the chair, I saw that it was too late. Mrs Wadham was dead.

But slowly, painfully, the girl Cynthia now began to emerge from the old woman: like a living creature struggling out of a chrysalis. She was shining so that I would have been afraid to touch her. For her face was alight with joy, in this last difficult separation she was incandescent with happiness.

From the old age crumpled in the chair, her radiant spirit passed through the wall and the glass, ran to him without marking the snow. It was bright morning now, but they were brighter than any morning on earth could be. I couldn't see their faces for the brightness, as they met – burned – vanished.

Further Red Fox titles that you might enjoy reading are listed on the following pages. They are available in bookshops or they can be ordered directly from us.

If you would like to order books, please send this form and the money due to:

ARROW BOOKS, BOOKSERVICE BY POST, PO BOX 29, DOUGLAS, ISLE OF MAN, BRITISH ISLES. Please enclose a cheque or postal order made out to Arrow Books Ltd for the amount due, plus 30p per book for postage and packing to a maximum of £3.00, both for orders within the UK. For customers outside the UK, please allow 35p per book.

NAME _____

ADDRESS _____

_____

Please print clearly.

Whilst every effort is made to keep prices low, it is sometimes necessary to increase cover prices at short notice. If you are ordering books by post, to save delay it is advisable to phone to confirm the correct price. The number to ring is THE SALES DEPARTMENT 071 (if outside London) 973 9700.

Other great reads from **Red Fox**

The Millennium books are novels for older readers from the very best science fiction and fantasy writers

---

A DARK TRAVELLING Roger Zelazny

An 'ordinary' 14-year-old, James Wiley has lost his father to a parallel world in the darkbands. With the help of his sister Becky, James, the exchange student and Uncle George, the werewolf, James goes in search of his parent.

ISBN 0 09 960970 3 £2.99

PROJECT PENDULUM Robert Silverberg

Identical twins Sean and Eric have been chosen for a daring experiment. One of them will travel into the distant past. The other into the distant future. And with each swing of the time pendulum they will be further apart . . .

ISBN 0 09 962460 5 £2.99

THE LEGACY OF LEHR Katherine Kurtz

The interstellar cruiser *Valkyrie* is forced to pick up four sinister, exotic cats, much to the captain's misgivings. His doubts appear justified when a spate of vicious murders appear on board.

ISBN 0 09 960960 6 £2.99

CHESS WITH A DRAGON David Gerrold

The Galactic InterChange was the greatest discovery in history . . . but now it had brought disaster. Unless Yake could negotiate a deal with the alien in front of him, mankind would be reduced to a race of slaves.

ISBN 0 09 960950 9 £2.99

Other great reads from *Red Fox*

Fantasy fiction—the Song of the Lioness series

ALANNA—THE FIRST ADVENTURE
Tamora Pierce

Alanna has just one wish—to become a knight. Her twin brother, Thom, prefers magic and wants to be a great sorcerer. So they swop places and Alanna, dressed as a boy, sets off for the king's court. Becoming a knight is difficult—but Alanna is brave and determined to succeed. And her gift for magic is to prove essential to her survival . . .

ISBN 0 09 943560 8   £3.50

IN THE HAND OF THE GODDESS
Tamora Pierce

Alan of Trebond is the smallest but toughest of the squires at court. Only Prince Jonathan knows she is really a girl called Alanna.

As she prepares for her final training to become a knight, Alanna is troubled. Is she the only one to sense the evil in Duke Roger? Does no one realise what a threat his steely ambition poses?

Alanna must use every ounce of her warrior skills and her gift for magic if she is to survive her Ordeal of Knighthood—and outwit the dangerous sorcerer duke.

ISBN 0 09 955560 3   £3.50

The third and fourth titles in the Song of the Lioness series, THE GIRL WHO RODE LIKE A MAN and LIONESS RAMPANT will be published by Red Fox in July 1992.

Other great reads ~~from **Red Fox**~~

Haunting fiction for older readers from Red Fox

THE XANADU MANUSCRIPT
John Rowe Townsend

There is nothing unusual about visitors in Cambridge.

So what is it about three tall strangers which fills John with a mixture of curiosity and unease? Not only are they strikingly handsome but, for apparently educated people, they are oddly surprised and excited by normal, everyday events. And, as John pursues them, their mystery only seems to deepen.

Set against a background of an old university town, this powerfully compelling story is both utterly fantastic and oddly convincing.

'An author from whom much is expected and received.' *Economist*

ISBN 0 09 975180 1   £2.99

ONLOOKER   Roger Davenport

Peter has always enjoyed being in Culver Wood, and dismissed the tales of hauntings, witchcraft and superstitions associated with it. But when he starts having extraordinary visions that are somehow connected with the wood, and which become more real to him than his everyday life, he realizes that something is taking control of his mind in an inexplicable and frightening way.

Through his uneasy relationship with Isobel and her father, a Professor of Archaeology interested in excavating Culver Wood, Peter is led to the discovery of the wood's secret and his own terrifying part in it.

ISBN 0 09 975070 8   £2.99

Other great reads from **Red Fox**

Leap into humour and adventure with Joan Aiken

Joan Aiken writes wild adventure stories laced with comedy and melodrama that have made her one of the best-known writers today. Her James III series, which begins with *The Wolves of Willoughby Chase*, has been recognized as a modern classic. Packed with action from beginning to end, her books are a wild romp through a history that never happened.

THE WOLVES OF WILLOUGHBY CHASE

Even the wolves are not more evil than the cruel Miss Slighcarp . . .

ISBN 0 09 997250 6   £2.99

BLACK HEARTS IN BATTERSEA

Dr Field invited Simon to London – so why can't Simon find him?

ISBN 0 09 988860 2   £3.50

THE CUCKOO TREE

Deadly danger for Dido as she comes up against black magic.

ISBN 0 09 988870 X   £3.50

DIDO AND PA

Why is there a man with a bandaged face hiding in the attic?

ISBN 0 09 988850 5   £3.50

MIDNIGHT IS A PLACE

Thrown out of his home, Lucas must find a way to live in the cruel town of Blastburn.

ISBN 0 09 979200 1   £3.50

Other great reads from **Red Fox**

Spinechilling stories to read at night

THE CONJUROR'S GAME Catherine Fisher

Alick has unwittingly set something unworldly afoot in Halcombe Great Wood.

ISBN 0 09 985960 2   £2.50

RAVENSGILL William Mayne

What is the dark secret that has held two families apart for so many years?

ISBN 0 09 975270 0   £2.99

EARTHFASTS William Mayne

The bizarre chain of events begins when David and Keith see someone march out of the ground . . .

ISBN 0 09 977600 6   £2.99

A LEGACY OF GHOSTS Colin Dann

Two boys go searching for old Mackie's hoard and find something else . . .

ISBN 0 09 986540 8   £2.99

TUNNEL TERROR

The Channel Tunnel is under threat and only Tom can save it . . .

ISBN 0 09 989030 5   £2.99

Other great reads from **Red Fox**

Superb historical stories from Rosemary Sutcliff

Rosemary Sutcliff tells the historical story better than anyone else. Her tales are of times filled with high adventure, desperate enterprises, bloody encounters and tender romance. Discover the vividly real world of Rosemary Sutcliff today!

THE CAPRICORN BRACELET
ISBN 0 09 977620 0 £2.50

KNIGHT'S FEE
ISBN 0 09 977630 8 £2.99

THE SHINING COMPANY
ISBN 0 09 985580 1 £3.50

THE WITCH'S BRAT
ISBN 0 09 975080 5 £2.50

SUN HORSE, MOON HORSE
ISBN 0 09 979550 7 £2.50

TRISTAN AND ISEULT
ISBN 0 09 979550 7 £2.99

BEOWULF: DRAGON SLAYER
ISBN 0 09 997270 0 £2.50

THE HOUND OF ULSTER
ISBN 0 09 997260 3 £2.99

THE LIGHT BEYOND THE FOREST
ISBN 0 09 997450 9 £2.99

THE SWORD AND THE CIRCLE
ISBN 0 09 997460 6 £2.99

Other great reads from **Red Fox**

THE WINTER VISITOR   Joan Lingard

Strangers didn't come to Nick Murray's home town in winter.
And they didn't lodge at his house. But Ed Black had—and Nick
Murray didn't like it.

Why had Ed come? The small Scottish seaside resort was
bleak, cold and grey at that time of year. The answer, Nick
begins to suspect, lies with his mother—was there some past
connection between her and Ed?

ISBN 0 09 938590 2   £1.99

STRANGERS IN THE HOUSE   Joan Lingard

Calum resents his mother remarrying. He doesn't want to move
to a flat in Edinburgh with a new father and a thirteen-year-old
stepsister. Stella, too, dreads the new marriage. Used to living
alone with her father she loathes the idea of sharing their small
flat.

Stella's and Calum's struggles to adapt to a new life, while
trying to cope with the problems of growing up are related with
great poignancy in a book which will be enjoyed by all older
readers.

ISBN 0 09 955020 2   £2.99